WINGS OF FIRE

G. BAILEY

Created with Vellum

MORE BOOKS BY G. BAILEY

HER GUARDIANS SERIES

HER FATE SERIES

PROTECTED BY DRAGONS SERIES

LOST TIME ACADEMY SERIES

THE DEMON ACADEMY SERIES

DARK ANGEL ACADEMY SERIES

SHADOWBORN ACADEMY SERIES

DARK FAE PARANORMAL PRISON SERIES

SAVED BY PIRATES SERIES

THE MARKED SERIES

CONTENTS

DESCRIPTION

Four lost dragon guards. Three choices. Two betrayals and one secret . . .

Dumped on earth with three dragon guards, who have no idea who Isola is, isn't what anyone had planned. With the biggest betrayal still haunting her heart, it's hard for Isola to remember what she has to do, and that she has to return to Dragca. Only making her dragons remember her, isn't as easy as she hoped. The three guards, who she knows it's forbidden to love, are doing everything to make sure they win her heart . . . . So, what could go wrong? With dreams of her betrayer literally haunting her, and the dangers of earth becoming a problem no one can protect her from, everything seems lost when it's dangerous to be.

The curse must fall, like fire for ice, betrayal and death must be the price . . .

This story follows the Her Guardian Universe from a new point of view.

PROLOGUE

Every step he makes to get closer to me is dangerous because of what I'm feeling, what I'm thinking. I don't want to lie to him, and yet, I can't let him closer. I can't tell him anything, but he doesn't remember enough to save himself. He pushes me further into the wall, his body pressed against mine. I close my eyes, knowing I can't be trusted to look at him.

"I know if I kiss you right now, you will taste as sweet as a peach and more addictive than anything I've ever tasted in my life," he growls, and I feel a finger tracing down my cheek, towards my neck. His hand slides to the back of my head, gripping my nape and angling my face towards his. Even then, I still don't open my eyes, not even when I feel his warm breath on my lips. I know he is inches away from me, and if he kisses me, I won't have the power to stop him. To fight what feels right.

"Open those eyes and tell me the truth," he urges, yet it feels like a demand. A dark, seductive one that sends shivers through me.

"I can't," I whisper, freezing when I feel his hand tighten on my neck, and his lips ever so gently brush mine.

"Soon then," he promises, and lets me go. He steps back, and I release the breath I'd been holding. I open my eyes, seeing him open the bedroom door and walk out without another word.

What the hell am I doing?

Fire must fall for ice, and ice must fall for fire. Evil and good must be equal. Not all evil is truly lost . . . remember, princess . . . not all evil is truly lost . . . .

"Melody?" I shake my head to clear the haze I've been in, looking around at the tiled ceiling, and feeling the cold from the floor I'm lying on. Everything I'd forgotten for the last . . . well, god knows how long, comes rushing back to me like a smack to the head. Thorne betrayed me. My father is dead. My dragon guard don't remember who they are, much less who I am. I shouldn't remember, but I do. I'm back on Earth, apparently in . . . school? *And I'm angry, so damn angry.* Ice shoots out of my hands, freezing the floor below me, and starts to spread. I

5

close my eyes, begging my dragon to calm down just a little. *We can't do anything now.*

"You're back? I was trapped," she whispers to me, her voice distant in my mind, even now.

"I'm back, and so are you," I confirm and shut her away to get some answers.

"Do you remember? I've never *quite* done that before," Melody says, her head appearing above my face as she stands and leans over me, her long black hair falling over her face. I remember her being my friend in one part of my mind, but then I remember her from my dreams and her voice from when she made me forget everything. She is the seer and a relative of mine. Holy crap, I've been friends with her for what I remember is a long time. Then I remember Elias, Dagan, and Korbin not recognizing me on the bus. She must have taken their memory, too. I don't know if I can trust her.

"You took them from me? And you've been in my dreams! Who the hell are you? You aren't Melody, my childhood friend," I shake my head, getting up off the floor as everything starts to get confusing. It's like two stories are playing in my head, the one where I grew up in this small town with Melody as a friend, and the other where I'm the princess of Dragca, who was seriously betrayed. I have to close my eyes, focusing on the princess story, my real-life story, so I don't get confused. She sighs, waving a hand over herself, and the black swirls of the seer marks appear on her face, and down her arms. Her jeans and crop top are replaced with a long red dress that looks amazing on her.

"My name really is Melody, but people I like call me Odie," she explains, and I just stare at her, gaping like a fish, before I snap myself out of it and walk away. She doesn't follow me, just watching as I go to the sink. I turn on the tap, getting a handful of water and splashing my face. I feel like I've just woken up from a long sleep. I dry my face with a paper towel, chucking it into the bin before turning to look at her. She is all I have left now, no other close family. Except my uncle, but I doubt he is still alive.

"I don't want to know about your name, Melody, who the hell are you to me? A cousin? An auntie? What are you?" I demand, getting frustrated. The happy look finally drops from her face, the seriousness of the moment appearing in her eyes.

"Your sister," she says quietly, a hint of sadness on her face as I step back, shaking my head.

"That's not possible," I say, knowing she can't possibly be my sister. She has to be a distant relative, not this. My parents wouldn't have lied to me like that.

"You're not stupid, Isola. You knew I had to be closely related to you in order to visit your dreams," she says. As she steps close to me, her body shimmers ever so slightly in the light.

"You're not really here, are you?" I ask, and she shakes her head.

"An illusion, one only you can see because we share blood. Others just have memories of me, but I'm not really here for them," she shrugs. "It's complicated magic. It took me months of reading about it in the royal library to learn how to appear solid and not ghost-like."

"Are you my father's daughter? Or my mother's?" I ask, needing to know which of my parents betrayed the other. Melody looks the same age as me, or she must be close, meaning one of my parents was a cheat.

"My mother was the last royal seer, and my father was the king," she says quietly, and I stare at her. She doesn't look a thing like me or my father, no blonde hair or pale-blue eyes, but there's something in the shape of her face. She gives me a look that reminds me of one my father would have when he was sad about something. I step back, looking away from her as pain spreads through me. He is dead, and we never really had any time together. All I have of my parents are lost memories and secrets, it seems. I lost the throne my father worked so hard to keep, I've failed him.

"I can't believe he betrayed my mother like that," I whisper in disbelief, shaking my head, and turning away from Melody. I can't even call him out on it, because he is dead. One of the last things he promised me was that I'm the only heir, that he never had any other children. It was all lies, plus he betrayed my sweet mother. She loved him, I remember that. I remember how they looked at each other, I thought it was love, but I guess no one really knows what goes on behind closed doors. A lot, apparently.

"I'm alone," I whisper, mildly panicking. That thought hurts more than all the other pain in my life, because it's so true. I can't even think about Thorne, not without wanting to walk through a portal, find him, and punch him straight in his good-looking face.

"No, you're not. I'm here, and you are all I have left, too," she says, and I turn to stare at her for a little while, both of us silent. We both share a father, who we recently lost, but she is still a stranger to me. I look at her, really look, and just see the confident friend that part of me thinks I've known for years. But I know that's not who she is, or at least, not *all* of her. The black, tattoo-like designs covering her arms and extending up her neck and cheeks remind me of who she really is. They meet in the middle of her forehead, curling at the ends. I don't remember her mother—only that she died at some point when I was still in Dragca, as a child. Melody is alone, too. I know that, but I still can't completely trust her.

"What is Thorne doing?" I ask her, needing to know if she is still in the castle, and what is going on back at home.

"Your stepbrother is . . . well, actually . . . his mother is making a lot of changes. We need you back, everyone thinks you're dead," she explains, biting her lip a little when snow starts falling from my hands again. It's only because I'm thinking about him, my anger is just too raw to control. I know I need to rein it in, though, when I see Melody's slightly worried face as she steps back from the ice spreading across the floor.

"I'm not going to hurt you," I tell her, and she laughs.

"You couldn't anyway, not without a big fight,

and I don't think we are those kinds of siblings. I'm more worried about Thorne," she says, and a flash of jealousy shoots out from my dragon. It overwhelms me, reminding me that she thinks of Thorne as hers. He never was; he's no treasure to hoard or collect, just a viper in a nest.

"I'm going to kill him when I see him next," I seethe, and she just smiles like she knows something I don't. I don't like it.

"Don't ask what you don't want to know, sister," she says, calling me sister like it's a normal thing. Not like it's the very first time she has called me that.

"Where is Bee? She was in the castle last I knew," I say, starting to panic, and I look down at my hand, seeing the tree mark. It looks normal, nothing's wrong with it. *Surely if something happened to her, I would know?*

"I have her. When you come to rescue me, you will get her back. She misses you and is getting powerful. Also, it's getting more difficult to hide her, trickier. I will protect her with my life because of who she is. She is all that is left of the light now." I'm relieved, but still a little worried. I watch as her eyes start to glow blue, and she shakes a little.

"Are you okay?" I ask her.

"I have to go, but you need to get the others to remember, and then sneak into Dragca with their help. Once they remember, they will know what to do," she says abruptly, and I turn to see her move closer, tilting her head to the side.

"Who?" I ask.

"Dagan, Elias, and Korbin. They need to remember who they are, so they can save you. Remember, sister, not everything is as it seems. There is only one way you will get them to remember. I just can't tell you how to do it," she says.

"Why not?" I demand.

"Because it would mess with fate, and fate has messed with you enough, Isola," she explains. Melody then gradually fades away, until I'm standing alone in the bathroom, surrounded by snow and ice. I walk over to the sink, the ice cracking under my boots. I stare at myself, inspecting the changes from the last time I saw myself. My hair is a lot longer, hitting my waist, and my face seems older and is covered in makeup. *Who wears so much of this crap?* I pick my bag up off the floor, putting it on the side. I open it up, seeing textbooks, a pencil case, and my phone inside. I flip my phone on, seeing that it is basically empty of texts or anything, but the date throws me off a little.

"Two thousand and nineteen," I say, dropping my phone back into my bag in shock. It's been two years since Thorne betrayed me; two years since I lost my father because of him. *How am I even still in school? I must be doing my A-levels now, and finishing school soon.* Two years . . . I swear I'm going to make him pay for every single day I've lost and so much more.

"Everything okay, Miss Dragice? You aren't usually late to my class," a teacher stops me as I walk past a classroom with its door open, so she can see me. There goes the plan of finding the guys and following them, okay, stalking them. *But stalking is okay if it's for their own good, or at least, that's what I'm telling myself.* I stop, turning to face the teacher who is tapping her foot on the floor with an unimpressed look. She is an older woman, with short grey hair tied at the back of her neck, and her skin is covered in wrinkles that pull across her face when she frowns at me. I remember her being a nice teacher, but the memory of the class is fading. I think it's history, no math? *I don't know.*

"Are you coming into class? Or just planning on

standing there staring?" she asks me, and I look at the doors of the school once more but look back at the teacher and decide maybe I need to act normal for a while. I doubt Thorne left me here alone, I bet someone here is a dragon in hiding or something, watching me for anything suspicious. Thorne is too smart to leave me on Earth without a guarantee that I wouldn't come back and kick his stupid ass off the throne.

"Sorry I'm late," I say, pulling my bag up on my shoulder and walking into the class. There are thirty or so students in here, and it's weird that I sort of remember them. It's like the memories of being here as a student and growing up in this town are stuck in my mind, but so is the actual truth. This is still the town I grew up in, this is the same school I went to with Jace. I swallow the bitterness I feel that he isn't here. That Esmeralda is still walking around free of punishment when she killed him. My vow to kill her, it just bothers me now because I know I won't be able to keep it for a while. I need to train, get much stronger, and somehow get the people of Dragca behind me, to get back my throne. I slide into my normal seat, two rows back, next to a girl named Hallie. Hallie winks at me, before looking back towards the front of class as the teacher starts talking about William Shakespeare. I suddenly remember this is my literature class, and that was what we were studying. It's all confusing and is slowly giving me a headache. *I guess that is what happens when someone messes with your head.*

"Everyone knows what we have been going over. With your upcoming test next week, I suggest you all start studying. Please come and see me if you have any problems," the teacher says, and everyone starts pulling their textbooks out of their bags. I get mine out, opening it up to the page I remember.

So weird that I remember the page, but not the teacher's name.

"How come you were late?" Hallie asks me, flipping through her own book. I look over at her, and scrutinize my friend. She has black hair, and currently has the tips dyed blue, though she changes the colour depending on her mood. She also covers her brown eyes with blue contacts; she hates wearing glasses and likes blue eyes. I remember meeting her when I was ten in the fake memory, but I also remember seeing her around school when I was here in my real life with Jace. We certainly weren't best friends like we are now, I didn't even know her name then. Yet, she is the only one that isn't fearful of me, like most human females are. I know everything about Hallie now, from her messed-up parents, to the two guys she's sleeping with that don't know about each other. She knows everything about me, too, all of the fake lie of a life anyway. The real me, the princess of Dragca, she knows nothing about. I feel a little guilty that she has been dragged into my mess of a life.

"Complicated," I say, rubbing my temples with my fingers and looking down. *Complicated is an understatement, but okay, that works.*

"Where is Odie?" she asks, meaning she still remembers my seer sister who was in school every day for as long as I can remember. I'd hoped Melody had made her forget, or done something. *Thanks, sister.*

"Erm . . . her family took her on holiday for a bit, and she's going to be gone at least a month," I say, making up the only excuse I can think of right now. It's one that gives me a fair amount of time to stalk the guys and make them remember.

"Lucky cow, the rest of us normal people have to put up with all this rain," she nudges my shoulder with hers, and then looks down at her book.

"Did you see the new students?" I ask her, needing to know where Elias, Dagan, and Korbin are. If anyone knows this school, and everything that is going on, it's Hallie.

"The ones that signed up today? Yeah, Issy, everyone has seen them. Hot damn, they are something else," she grins, pretending to cool herself down with her hand. Clearing her throat, the teacher stares at us, and we both look down pretending to read quietly. After a while, a student walks up to her, distracting her enough for us to continue talking.

"So . . . they aren't in classes today?" I muse.

"Nope, the rumour is they had to fill out paperwork or something, and they start tomorrow," she says, and snaps her head to the side to look at me with wide eyes, "Why? Is the ice queen finally thawing and crushing on someone?" she asks, making me tense up.

"What did you call me?" I ask.

"Ice queen, because you turn down every dude in school," she rolls her eyes at me, and I relax a little bit, "Come on, everyone calls you that. They are idiots, though."

"Maybe," I say, and look down at my own book, wanting to drop the subject. It's no use continuing to talk about them if they aren't even here today. I need to stalk them, like "find their house and then follow them around" kind of stalk. The normal stalking that won't get me arrested.

"I'm sure they will be invited to Michael's party in three weeks, he has an empty house again," she wags her eyebrows. I hate Michael. I hate him now, and I hated him when Jace and I went to school here. He is a jackass, who thinks his good looks mean everyone wants him, and he assumes, for some reason, that I want to sleep with him. It doesn't help that humans here on Earth are naturally attracted to female dragons; it's something to do with the pheromones in our scent. All I remember doing is turning down guys and watching their heartbroken ex-girlfriends glare at me. Hopefully, if I can get Elias, Dagan, or Korbin to be friends with me, then I should be left alone. Male dragons have the complete opposite effect on most humans, they want to avoid them. I doubt the girls here will listen to their instincts when they see the guys; they are all way too hot to evade. I hold back a growl, the thought of anyone touching them makes me want to punch something

"I doubt Michael will want competition there," I say, looking down at my hand where my nails are slowly turning to ice. Sliding my hands under the table, I make sure to keep my eyes down, just in case they turn silver. Dammit, I've got to control my emotions better than this. I did it for years with Jace, I can do it now. Taking a deep breath, I turn the page of my book and pretend to be interested in what it says.

"He would do anything for you, just ask him to invite them to the party. Then, being the good friend I am, I will distract Michael," she suggests. I start to tell her no when I realise I need to get close to the guys again, to make them trust me. It's going to be difficult in this school to do that. No, I need to make friends with them outside of school, and then figure out how to make them remember.

"Sounds like a plan," I say with a grin and start reading my textbook, hoping the day will go quickly.

CHAPTER
THREE

ISOLA

"Jules?" I call when I open my front door. I almost freeze when I see her come out of the kitchen, holding a bowl, and mixing something inside it with a spoon. She looks just like the last time I saw her, her grey hair up in a bun, and she's wearing an older-style dress with a flower and bird pattern. She looks like home, of all the memories I have of her. She wore a similar dress the first time I met her. I remember walking into this house, the dragon guards leaving me at the door, and she made me cookies as I cried. She didn't baby me, but she still comforted me. Since that day, she has always been there for me. I wasn't the best to her in the last couple of years before Jace died and I left for Dragca. I threw parties and got drunk all the time.

21

Overall, I was a total brat, but she didn't quit on me when most would have.

"Hello, darling, I'm making pumpkin pie for dessert, and your favourite casserole for dinner tonight," she says, and I smile tightly at her. I wonder how much magic it took for my sister to erase Jules's memory of me disappearing and to erase her memory of Jace, who she adored. What's more, how much magic did it take to make the whole town forget, to erase everyone's memories?

"Thanks. I have homework to do," I nod my head at the stairs, smiling tightly as my emotions begin to strangle me.

"Okay!" she says with a happy grin, not noticing my mood at all. She walks out of the room, heading back towards the kitchen. I run up the stairs, taking a deep breath when I get to my room. I feel like everything is piling up on top of me as I look around. It's my room, but it's not. There's no familiarities in here anymore, just plain bed sheets, piles of books that don't look read, and tiny holes in the walls where photos of Jace and me used to hang. Pressing my back against the door, I slide down and wrap my arms around my legs. I rest my head on my knees, trying to calm my breathing and stop the tears streaming down my face. It doesn't work; tears continue to fall without my permission as memories begin to overwhelm me, and I remember everything. Every memory of my time in Dragca is different now, my view on everything skewed. Every moment with Thorne is fake; he was lying, tricking me from the start, and I fell for it. He burnt Jace's body, was with me in that final moment that I will never forget, and now it's tainted with Thorne's betrayal. Our every moment spent together is soiled, when he opened up to me about his adoptive family and the reason for his animosity with Elias, when he taught me how to use my dragon sight, and when he was just there for me so many times. I scream into my hands, so angry that he did this to me. *The lying bastard.*

"Isola, can you come down?" I hear Jules shout, making me snap out of it. I can't allow myself to break down; I don't have the luxury of wallowing in my despair. Elias, Dagan, Korbin, Melody, Bee, and the people of Dragca need me. I'm no princess, no leader if I sit here and cry about my problems. No, I need to get up and make a plan of action. I quickly sit up, wiping my eyes and checking I don't look too upset in the mirror. Opening the door, I walk down the corridor to the stairs, following the noise I can hear into the kitchen. I stop, nearly tripping on thin air when I see Dagan, Elias, and Korbin sitting at the table. They don't even look my way, just continue to talk, and I slowly walk up to Jules as she puts a casserole into the oven.

"My brother called, and apparently, his nephews need a place to stay for the next month or so. I don't know everything, but they are enrolled in school. I emailed your father, who replied saying it was fine," she explains, and I tighten my fists, knowing it couldn't have been my father who replied.

"Okay," I reply slowly, and she looks up, a slightly dazed expression on her face. Someone has been messing with her memories. Jules doesn't have any family, I remember her telling me that. It's why she made the perfect nanny for me and Jace growing up.

"They are very good-looking, so it's best you don't go looking. Teenage pregnancies are no fun," she says nonchalantly. I choke on air, coughing a few times as I plainly nod at her. I didn't expect her to say that.

"You don't have to worry about that," I explain to her, and she winks.

"Sure, I don't," she looks at the guys, and I hear her mumble under her breath, "If only I was forty years younger." I laugh a little, and then pull her to me, hugging her side.

"What was that for?" she asks.

"I just missed you."

"You haven't had a chance to miss me, we see each other every day," she says as I pull away. "Now go and say hello to your roommates, silly girl." I nod at her before looking back at the guys. It's weird to see them in jeans and normal polo shirts. Elias still has a leather jacket on, so some things don't change, but it's clear a lot has. I look at Dagan next, noticing his black hair is a little longer than before, but the sides are still shaved, and he still has his lip ring. Korbin and Elias have also grown their hair out, it falls close to their eyes now and just adds to the wild look they both have. I wonder where their dragons are, they must be inside of them somewhere, but just hidden. My sister must be insanely powerful to do what she has, to make everyone forget, and to even appear as an illusion. I wonder if she has a dragon inside of her, as she is half ice dragon after all, and it could boost her power. Maybe her dragon blood makes her seer powers that much stronger. *I guess I have a lot of things to ask her when I see her next.*

"Well, go and say hello to them, they will be your roommates for a while. Besides, staring is rude," she chastises, shoving me towards them. I take a deep breath, telling myself I can act normal and like I don't know them as I walk to their table. They look up, one by one, until they are all staring at me. It's odd for them to stare at me like this, like I'm a total stranger to them. Their eyes assess me, rolling over my body and making me shiver. Their total attention is on me, three powerful, sexy dragons, and they all look at me like they have just found a treasure they want.

"I'm Isola," I say, after clearing my throat a little and sliding my fingers into the back of my jeans. Dagan leans back in his seat, his eyes still travelling over my body while moving his lip ring and grins.

"I-Sol-A," he spells my name out slowly, wickedly, and then chuckles.

"Dagan, right?" I ask him, and he nods, biting his lip a little and giving me a strange look. I look away before I can try to decipher that look, it's not a look of remembrance, that's for sure.

"And you're Korbin?" I ask Korbin, hating that I have to pretend not to know. He isn't even looking at me anymore, and I notice straight away that he no longer has his beard. Damn, I liked that beard on him. Korbin ignores me completely, choosing to mess on his phone instead. *Great.*

"I'm Elias, and no, I don't want you to sneak into my room later," Elias says, winking at me as he gets up and pulls his cigarette packet out of his jacket. His hair is longer, making him have to brush it out of his eyes. It makes him look wilder, more untameable, and honestly, so sexy I'm having trouble not reaching up to touch it.

"Those things kill humans," I say, repeating a warning I once gave him to see if it jogs his memory, but it doesn't seem to have any impact. He just shrugs and puts the cigarette in his mouth.

"Usually the best things in life do kill us, princess," he says, making my heart pound as he walks past me and to the back door.

"Princess?" I ask, wondering if he remembers calling me it.

"You look like a princess, a naughty one at that," he chuckles darkly, walking out as I smile. He might not remember who I am exactly. None of them do, but I have hope because of those two words. There's only one dragon that calls me naughty princess, and I intend to make sure he remembers me.

FOUR

THORNE

"Is it done?" I ask Melody, shutting her door behind me and turning to look at her. She is sitting on a window seat, a crystal ball in her hand and her black hair draping around it until she sits back. The seers' rooms are just as grand as the rest of the castle, and it makes me uncomfortable. I look around at the gold walls, the gold floors, and gold linen hanging everywhere. I didn't grow up like this, I grew up in a muddy hut in the forest. The nicest thing we had was a small, wooden, dragon knight toy I used to play with. Melody is used to this, and yet, I hate it. It's a castle full of lies, secrets, and is dripping with blood.

"Come and see, my King," she says formally, yet

the twitch of her lips tells me she is being sarcastic. I walk over, looking down into the crystal ball as it glimmers before Isola appears. She is in a kitchen, talking to Dagan, Korbin, and Elias by the looks of it. Her blonde hair is much longer than it's ever been, soft-looking, and falling in curls down her back. She looks up, almost as if she can sense us looking, and I get to see her pale-blue eyes, doll-like features, and pale skin. It hurts to see her when I know how much she must hate me. I just want to be by her side, able to protect her in the open rather than in secret, behind her back. She has good reason to hate me, and I doubt she will ever forgive me, or let me even be her friend after all I've done. But I will protect her and ensure she lives through this.

"How long until she can make them remember?" I ask Melody. She waves a hand over the ball, making it go cloudy, and slides off the seat.

"I don't know, I've seen it happen but not the time or date," she admits.

"We don't have long! When my mother goes to the dungeons and sees Dagan, Elias, and Korbin are free . . ." I trail off, looking away from her. I doubt any of us will live when she figures out I've betrayed her, that I chose Isola over her. It's not that I don't love my mother or want the crown, it's just that I know it's what needs to be done. The curses need to end, Isola needs the throne to protect her. *I'm no king if I betray everyone to have the crown.*

"I know. I know she will find her guards, but I've told you before I don't know what happens after that. My visions aren't all seeing," she says, her frustration clear in her voice.

"Fine, I should go in case someone comes looking for me," I say, walking to the door, but her voice stops me.

"You should tell her how you feel, what you did to save her. Maybe more importantly, what you didn't do, Thorne," she tells me gently. I look back, locking eyes with her blue ones as she folds her hands and waits for me to reply. Melody looks nothing like her sister, yet they have the same demanding nature. It must run in the family or something.

"She *should* hate me. I might have fixed some things, but I still betrayed her," I say emotionlessly, not even able to say her name out loud. That betrayed look she gave me before she lost her memory, it haunts me, leaving me unable to sleep. I can't get it out of my head, and I know it's my fault, I brought it on myself. I wish I could have warned her, told her how things had changed for us all, and how I had changed my mind when I saw her father die. But being completely honest with myself, the plan changed the moment I met Isola Dragice.

"When you see her, you won't be able to fool yourself or her. She will figure it out, considering only one person could have saved her dragon guards and kept her alive," she suggests.

"I will always keep her alive, nothing will ever mean more to me than her life," I snap, reining my dragon in as it flares to life, wanting to go to Isola, to protect her.

"Minnnneee," my dragon demands, his claim on Isola is overwhelming because of what I did. When I open my eyes, Melody is staring at me with what looks like sympathy written all over her face.

"Here," Melody says, walking over to a box next to her bed and pulling out a bracelet. It's all black stones, but I don't have a clue what it is or does. She comes over, handing it to me.

"What is it?" I ask.

"Wear it when you sleep, and you will understand. It's a gift, a rare one, so don't lose it. I want it back," she says and then nods her head at the door.

"You should go," she tells me. I don't question her, just open the door and walk out, slipping the bracelet onto my wrist as I go. I walk down the grand corridors of the castle, intending to go to my rooms, when my mother walks out of one of the royal rooms. She smiles at me and walks over, placing her hand on my shoulder. My mother has clearly just woken up, her blonde hair is down, and she has a cloak on over her dress. Nothing like the white leather she usually wears and comes back to the castle with blood spots all over.

"Where have you been so early, son?" she asks, and walks next to me as I keep going. I hate that I have to lie to her, betray her, but I know it's the right thing to do. My mother isn't who she used to be, and it's the king's fault for making her like this. Evil in a way, but I can save her. I will save her and Isola, but not without the price of having them both hate me.

"Just a walk to the kitchens, I was hungry," I say, and her dark-blue eyes look up at me. They used to be clear blue, like most ice dragons, but over the years they have gotten darker. Now they are so dark, you can barely see the blue, it's almost black. The black would match the black veins crawling up her arms, but I try not to think about it and look away.

"I have to leave the castle with Esmeralda today, we have a job to finish in the north," she explains.

"What job? I should come with you," I ask,

curious and desperate to keep an eye on her before she destroys the entire kingdom. I don't know what she is doing, but she comes back covered in black dust, and smelling of fire.

"Nothing for you to worry about, and I told you before, you can't leave the castle. You're the king, and until you are mated, with an heir on the way, it's too dangerous for you," she says, sighing.

"I'm not mating anytime soon. I've told you this," I say, trying to hide my annoyance that she won't tell me what she is doing.

"When the seers are back on our side, or Melody tells us who your future mate is, we will find her," she says, like it's no concern for her. Melody pretends to help her all the time, but I doubt she is helping her much.

"The seers still won't come here?" I ask.

"No, but they will change their minds very soon," she smiles as we get to my room.

"What are you going to do? You can't just kill everyone that doesn't side with you, mother," I warn her, and dark lines crawl down her cheeks for just a second before she shakes her head.

"I won't kill *them*," she says sweetly and walks away. I open the doors to my room, walking across it and straight to the balcony. I have to take deep breaths to calm my dragon down as I look over the mountains as the suns shine above them. I look over at the crown on the side. It's a worthless trinket, considering I have no idea what is going on outside of this castle.

A king with no power is no king at all.

CHAPTER
FIVE
ISOLA

"*I*sola," *a voice whispers, the voice both hauntingly familiar and heartbreaking. My mind knows who it is, without me even having to look.*

"*Hello?*" *I ask, blinking my eyes open. All I see is smoke all around me. There is a fire in the background, and I quickly turn around, looking for the voice. Part of me doesn't want to find the man who spoke, but a deeper part of me still yearns for him.*

"*Here,*" *the voice says from behind me, and I spin, seeing a shadow of a man in the smoke.*

"*I can't see you,*" *I say, and he chuckles.*

"*You don't want to, you hate me,*" *he says sadly, but then still steps forward into the clearing. Thorne stands still as I get a good look at him. His ice-blue eyes lock with mine, his hair matching the stolen white crown on his head. I can't get used to the blonde hair, as I'm so used to seeing it brown. It has been kept short and suits his face more this way. He has a new outfit, still black leather and similar to his guard uniform, but this one is much nicer. He has a long cloak draped around him, with blue and red dragons stitched down the sides.*

"Of course I hate you, you killed my father! The very crown you wear, you stole from his dead body! You betrayed me! Get out of my head, and fuck off, you bastard!" I shout at him, stepping back when he steps closer. I'm literally shaking with anger, wishing this dream was real, so I could kill him.

"I can't escape you anymore than you can escape me, but hate me all you want," he whispers, and I barely even hear him as I go over the million different ways I could kill him. I think stabbing him through the heart like he did my father would be the best way. When he only stares at me, not saying anything, I have to reply.

"What the hell does that mean, Thorne?" I snap, and he strides quickly towards me. I back away until I can feel the heat from the fire burning my back. He grabs my face with his hands, pulling me towards me. I hit him, struggling to get away, and even try to call my ice, but it doesn't work.

"Fight me, hate me, but you can't shut me out, Issy,

and when you know why, you won't want to," he tells me and leans down, brushing his lips across my forehead. He lets go, allowing me to fall into the smoke.

"I hate you, don't come to me again. I have my dragon guards now," I shout, falling still but not fighting. The smoke takes me away from him, and that's what I want more than anything.

"I sent them to you, protected them for you, but that doesn't mean you shouldn't hate me, Issy," is the last thing I hear him say before everything feels like it is burnt away until only emptiness is left.

I SIT STRAIGHT UP in bed as my alarm blares, covered in sweat and with my heart pounding. Feeling my hand burning, I look at my tree mark and find it glowing red, before it gradually fades back to its normal green colour. When my heart stops pounding in my ears, and I calm down, I realise the dream couldn't be real. *It's just a bad dream, Thorne wasn't really there.* I turn my alarm off, seeing the display saying it's six in the morning, and I lean across the bed, switching my lamp on. Thorne can't contact me, it's impossible for him to do that across worlds, and I doubt he is on Earth. He might be a fire and ice dragon, but the only way to get into someone's dreams is to be a seer and have a blood connection, as far as I know. Thorne and I don't have any connection, so clearly, I'm just losing my mind. My laptop sits open beside me, I must have fallen asleep looking at it last night. Closing it, I look around my room again. I can't help the feeling that someone has taken a part of me, not just everything related to my previous life here. It's not just the photos of me and Jace that are missing, though that's a huge part of it. Anything related to Dragca is gone, all of the books, and it makes me wish I had read them now. Even my phone is different, it's not the one I had before, and that means the last image I have of Jace is just gone.

"Dammit," I swear, wiping the tears away, and knowing I can't be weak like this. I have three of the most stubborn men I've ever met to convince that they are dragons. *God, they are going to think I'm insane.*

"*Need to fly soon,*" my dragon whispers into my mind as I slide out of bed.

"*I know, I will find a way to sneak away tonight,*" I explain, and I feel her comfort at my words before I take over again. I don't need anyone seeing my eyes turning silver right now; that will freak them out. I grab my running clothes, after washing up in the bathroom, and then plait my hair without looking at my reflection for too long. I look just like my father, and I keep imagining him, how disappointed he must be in me. *What would he say if he were alive? How would he save Dragca?* I leave my room, looking at the other five doors down the corridor. I know Jules moved into the room opposite me, leaving the three rooms and the shared bathroom at the end of the corridor for the guys. Her and my rooms have their own bathroom; I guess the guys don't mind sharing theirs. It stings that she is sleeping in Jace's room now, and I know if I went in there, it wouldn't be anything like it used to be. His books wouldn't be littered around, and his guitar wouldn't be leaning against the messy bed. This house feels like it's haunting me more than the messed-up dream of Thorne. Even his name annoys me, I hate him so much. I shake my head, moving away from my door, and walk down the corridor. Instead of dwelling on the past, or things I can't change, I decide to focus on my plans for the day.

"Good morning!" I say, walking into the kitchen and yawning slightly. Korbin is sitting on a stool, and his head lifts up, locking those green eyes with mine. I knew he would be up early. I miss the smiles he used to give me, and even almost miss our runs and his threats to throw fireballs at my ass if I didn't speed up. He doesn't say anything as he gets up, he just walks over to me and reaches his hand out to get something out of my hair. He pulls back, showing me a little feather.

"It must be the feather duvet I sleep on," I say, and he smirks, brushing the feather down my cheek slowly and almost seductively, making me shiver all over.

"Maybe you should show it to me," his husky voice suggests, sending goosebumps up and down my body. Korbin has never spoken to me like this, and part of me doesn't want him to stop. I trace my eyes over his tight pajama shirt and snug shorts that show off his muscular thighs. *Who knew thighs could be attractive?*

"My duvet?" I ask confused, and he shakes his head, stepping closer to me. We are only a breath apart when he whispers.

"Your bed, doll." My mouth parts in shock, and he steps back, leaving me a little shaky. He picks his phone up off the side and acts like nothing just happened.

"I-I don't think that's—" I start to say, stumbling over my words and acting like a timid little girl that's never spoken to a guy before. *Damn it, get it together, Isola.*

"We could always start off with a date," he suggests, his deep and husky voice making me just want to listen to him talk forever. I don't reply to his flirting. I can't let my hormones control me, not right now, anyway. I need him to be my friend again, we can't risk anything else. It's too dangerous. The fact they don't know about their dragons doesn't mean a thing, they would lose their dragons permanently by falling for me. Or me for them. I don't really know specifics on how the curse works, but I'm not going to test it. Not only would they hate me forever, but I'd hate myself.

"Do you run? I like to run every morning," I say, lying my ass off. I spent most of the night reading about how to jog someone's memory. One of the most successful recommendations is to get them back into their routine. *That means running, oh god, running.*

"I usually run in the evenings, but a pretty little doll like you shouldn't be running on your own," he says, walking past me and towards the stairs. "Get us some water while I get changed."

"Alright," I reply, and he runs up the stairs. I walk to the fridge, pulling out two bottles of water. I head for the door, putting the water down to pull on my trainers. Hearing steps on the staircase, I turn and see Jules coming down. She has jeans and a long tunic shirt on today, and her hair is down. She looks happy, although slightly shocked.

"Wow . . . I didn't expect to see you down here already. Are you feeling okay?" she asks, knowing I don't like mornings. I usually roll out of bed with half an hour to spare, and still spend most of that time reading, before dragging my ass to the bus stop.

"I decided I need to be healthier. I'm going to run every morning with Korbin," I explain, and she chuckles.

"I bet seeing that boy in tight workout clothes and dripping with sweat has nothing to do with your need to be healthy and wake up earlier?" she says, making me choke on thin air, again, as she keeps laughing.

"I used to be young once, I'll have you know. I would have done more than run every morning to get close to a body like that," she teases, winking at me. She walks into the kitchen as I just stare after her in shock. Thankfully, Korbin comes running down the stairs, distracting me from thoughts of what Jules was like when she was younger. With all these comments lately, I'd bet she was a wild one. I try to not appreciate how amazing Korbin looks in his tight running shorts and loose shirt, but I majorly fail. *Holy crap on a cracker, he looks hot.* I trail my eyes over him shamelessly, and when I finally look into his eyes, he knows I've been checking him out. Thankfully, he doesn't call me on it. *I have no excuse.*

"Ready?" he asks gruffly, and I hand him his water as he gets closer.

"Yep," I respond. I need to use this time alone with him to make him remember, though I'm not sure how.

"Do you know a good route with a path?" he asks when we get outside, the cold morning air making me shiver. It's freezing out. The sun is just rising in the sky, but I know running will warm us up until the sun is fully out. Our house is in the middle of the woods, with a private driveway that leads down to a secluded road. There aren't any other houses for miles, and the only vehicle that comes this way is the school bus. The woods have a track I used to walk with Jace sometimes.

"Yeah, see over there," I point at the post in between the trees to the right, "there's a path all the way around the land and back," I explain.

"We should race. If I win, I get a date with you. If I lose," he pauses, "well, what would you like?"

"Nothing, I'm not taking that bet. We can't date," I say.

"Boyfriend? I should have guessed," he asks, disappointed.

"No boyfriend," I say, and he grins, his green eyes shining with the reflection of the sunrise.

"Then you best think of something you want to win, not that you really need to worry. You won't win anyway . . . I want that date," he tells me and takes off running. I run after him, cursing him with his green eyes and sexy voice for distracting me.

"It's cheating to have a head start!" I shout, and he looks back at me for a second, still keeping up his fast pace.

"I don't play fair, doll," he tells me, and I shake my head as I hustle to catch up to him. We run at a normal pace for most of the run. Then, in the last fifteen minutes of our race, he suddenly speeds up, and it's impossible for me to keep up with his pace. I swear under my breath when he quickly disappears from view, and I sprint as fast as I can to the end of the track. When I get there, Korbin is leaning against a tree, drinking water. I stand there gawking as it drips down his chin onto his chest, I can't help myself. In my distracted state, I trip on something and slam onto the ground. Nothing hurts, well my ego does, but I ignore that as I roll onto my back.

"Shit, here," I hear Korbin say, and he picks me up, letting me straighten myself out. He lifts his hand, picking some leaves out of my hair, and then pushing a strand behind my ear. I don't know what gets into me when he rests his hand on my cheek, but I lean my head into it. I close my eyes for a second and just breathe in his smoky scent. He might not know he is a dragon, but he still smells like one. He still has that comforting scent. When I open my eyes, Korbin is staring at me with such longing and desire, that I can't look away. Something is changing between us. I should stop it, I should run away from it . . . but I don't feel like I can.

"There's something about you, doll, and I want to know what it is," he whispers.

"There's nothing," I answer, wanting to say there's nothing that I can tell him.

"Nothing is definitely not a word I'd use to describe you, you are everything but it," he claims forcefully, sliding his hand from my cheek to my jaw, his thumb lightly skimming across my lips.

"You're a shameless flirt," I say, smiling a little

tensely. Pulling away, I wipe the dirt off myself and lean down to pick up my water bottle.

"Not usually, but with you, yes," he replies, watching me carefully as I try to shake off what just happened. *What happened to making him remember? This run accomplished nothing.*

"We should shower before school," I say, walking towards the house, and he swiftly catches up.

"I'm going to guess that wasn't an invite to shower together," he drawls.

"Nope," I giggle.

"I can wait. Our date is Saturday at seven," he says, running ahead of me and into the house before I can even say no. *Damn cocky dragon.*

CHAPTER
SIX
ISOLA

"Want a ride?" Elias's sexy voice drifts over to me, making me jump as I walk out of the house. I turn, seeing him sitting on a massive motorbike, and I have to make my eyes pull away from his leather-covered body. *Holy crap, he looks hot.* I only know it's Elias from his voice, as I can't see his face under his helmet, but I know he can see me ogling him.

"You have a motorbike . . . of course you do," I mutter, pulling my coat tighter around me as I glance up at the dark skies. Dagan and Korbin walk past, going down the drive to the bus stop, looking between Elias and me.

"It's going to rain before the bus gets here in half an hour, you should take the ride," Korbin suggests.

Dagan doesn't say a word, only staring at me intensely, like he is trying to figure out a puzzle.

"Make your choice, princess," Elias says. I shake my head, knowing I must be mad, and I walk over to Elias. He offers me a spare helmet, and I slide it on before getting onto the back of the bike. It's a little awkward to get on, being that I've never ridden one before, but I do manage. *Just not very gracefully.*

"You will need to hang on," his voice comes loudly through the helmet, and I realise they must have some kind of walkie-talkie built in them. I'm sure there's a technical word for it, but it just reminds me of the walkie-talkies we used to have as kids. I tentatively wrap my hands around his waist, trying not to feel the flat, hard muscles that are under my grip. He grabs my arms, making me slide forward on the seat until my body is wrapped around his, and he pulls my hands tighter around him. Elias starts the bike, and I close my eyes as it purrs to life underneath me. We begin to move, flying down the driveway by the sound and feel of it. It's scary at the start, but once I relax, it's pretty enjoyable. I'm used to flying or moving fast, it's what dragons do but at much higher heights. I'm still not looking though; my eyes are staying shut.

"Are you going to open your eyes?" Elias asks me after we round a corner.

"Nope," I reply back, and I hear him laugh through the helmet. It's oddly relaxing to hear his laugh, hear him so relaxed and happy.

"It's not that bad, you might like it if you try," he says, and I gently open one eye and then the next. We are driving through town; the shops and people seem like blurs, and it's incredible.

"It's so weird, but in a good way," I say, and he laughs, not replying to me. It's another ten minutes until we are pulling up to the school car park, and he stops his bike right near the front of the school. I get off, ignoring the stares from everyone as I pull my helmet off and hand it to Elias. He puts both of them in the space under the seat, and then unzips his riding gear. As he pulls it off, his shirt rides up, so I get a glance of his tattoos and the v shape that disappears into his jeans. He puts the outfit in the bike, and grabs his leather jacket, putting it on before slipping his keys into his pocket.

"Are you going to show me around then?" Elias asks after I spend way too long gaping at him. *Shit.*

"Yeah, sure, so where are you guys from?" I ask, and we start walking up the steps to the front doors. I need to know where they have been for the last two years and why Thorne said he brought them here. I can't accept that he did, that he helped me in any kind of way.

"A little bit of everywhere, our parents like to travel, but we are stuck here for a while," he explains, and I wonder who Melody made him think his parents are. I doubt they were travelling anywhere, either. Thorne's words keep rolling around in my mind. He claimed he kept them safe, so they must have been near him. Maybe they were kept in the castle or something.

"So, down here are all the classrooms, and at the end of this hall is the lunch room. On the right is the head teacher's office, the reception rooms, and to the left are the toilets," I say, pointing in each direction as I explain them. He nods, looking around as students walk past us, all watching him. He pulls a piece of paper out of his pocket, looking at the table on it.

"I have double English first, what about you?" he asks.

"Same," I say, and nod my head down the corridor, "it's this way."

"Isola!" I hear my name shouted, and turn around to see Michael running over to me. Michael has golden-blond hair and a massive build from all the training he does for football. He towers over me when he steps near me.

"Hey, Michael," I reply briskly, wanting to get to class. I need the time to spend thinking of new ways to get the guys to remember me.

"I heard from Hallie that you're finally coming to one of my parties at the end of the month?" he asks, stepping closer. I look over as Elias wraps an arm around my waist, pulling me to his side.

"We will be coming, I'm Elias," Elias says tensely, holding out a hand for Michael. Michael looks between us, anger flashing over his face, but he instantly schools his expression, shaking Elias's hand.

"You should come and train for the football team, I'm the captain. You have two brothers, right?" he asks.

"He does," Dagan's cold voice comes from behind Michael, just moments before he and Korbin step next to Elias and me.

"Cool. Anyway, can't wait to see you at the party . . . and your friends can come, too," he says, confusing me a little. I flinch when he steps closer, wrapping his arms around me as he pulls me away from Elias and drags me to his chest. I swear I hear someone growl, and I can only hope it was one of the guys and their dragon.

"We are going to be late for class," Dagan says, and you can hear the hostile tone in his voice. Michael lets go, grinning at me before walking away.

"Who is that?" Elias asks.

"Just this guy that goes to school here: Michael," I reply. All the guys watch Michael until he gets to his classroom and disappears from view. I place my hand on Elias's shoulder.

"We really will be late for class," I say, not really caring about being late, but I know I need to distract him from whatever he is thinking. Dagan and Korbin look at me once more before walking off, and Elias steps closer, putting his arm around my waist.

"What are you doing?" I ask, though I don't push him away. This close, I notice he still carries the smoky scent of his fire dragon, and it makes me want to press myself closer to him.

"*Mine,*" my dragon whispers, and Elias's eyes widen in surprise. He grabs my chin to look at me closely as I feel my eyes fade back to their normal blue. He saw them turn silver, he must have.

"Let go," I demand, and he narrows his eyes at me.

"Your eyes, they changed colour," he exclaims.

"You're seeing things, Elias," I reply nervously.

"Don't lie to me, I don't like it," he demands and lets go, stepping back and shaking his head.

"Eli?" I whisper, watching him hold his hands to his head for a few moments. When he finally looks back at me, he seems so lost.

"Class. We need to go to class, and then we *will* have a long chat tonight," he orders. "I don't like lies," he repeats, and I turn around, walking the rest of the way to class.

"I know, but I don't have any choice," I whisper to myself.

CHAPTER
SEVEN
ISOLA

"Issy, come on, we are going shopping, remember?" Hallie asks as soon as I step out of our final class. I feel Dagan, Elias, and Korbin follow me from the room. Someone has arranged it so we all have the same classes together. Probably the same person who made it possible for them to live with me. Something is going on, and I'm starting to feel like a puppet on a string, yet I don't know who it is that is controlling me. The guys haven't spoken to me much, not even at lunch, though they sat eating their food next to Hallie and me. It's awkward between us all, but I'm clueless as to why it feels that way.

"What?" I ask her, snapping out of my thoughts.

"Shopping? We made plans to go tonight," she

says, and I vaguely remember making plans with her in my fake life last week.

"Alright," I concede. When I drop the book I'm holding, I stop to pick it up, and someone slams into me. We both fall to the floor, and I land on something hard. I open my eyes to see Dagan underneath me, his hands on my waist and a serious expression clouding his eyes.

"Are you always this clumsy?" he asks. This moment reminds me of when we first met, how he jumped on me to save me back then. Not that he is saving me this time, but still.

"No . . . well, yes. I mean, I can be. I try not to be if that helps," I grin, and he shakes his head at me as I get off of him.

"Here," he hands me my book, but doesn't let go. He stands there, still staring at me with confusion written all over his face.

"Thanks, Dagan," I say, as he finally lets go of the book and steps away, rolling his lip ring. He always does that when he's thinking about something.

"No problem, kitty cat, see you at home," he replies and turns around, walking over to where Korbin and Elias are waiting for him by the door.

"'At home'? What have you not been telling me?" Hallie gasps dramatically, pushing her long hair behind her shoulders. I sigh, watching the guys disappear through the doors.

"They all moved in yesterday. Apparently, they need a place to stay for a while, and Jules is completely okay with it," I say, and her eyes widen. I walk to my locker, letting her process the shock, and shove my textbooks inside, before closing it to face her.

"Holy fucking shit!" Hallie exclaims, whacking my arm and making me laugh. I actually like this girl.

"Please, please say you're going to sneak into at least one of their rooms . . . like naked, so they can't resist," she begs, and I laugh.

"I don't think I need to do that, Besides, I have a date with Korbin on Saturday. It's a long story, but I kind of lost a bet," I tell her.

"Then we definitely need to find you something tight and sexy to wear," she wraps an arm around me and leads me to the door. We go in Hallie's car to the shopping centre, parking up and walking in. I look at Hallie, trying to find something from our fake past to ask her about. It's getting harder to remember, the memories becoming more distant.

"Are your mum and dad still arguing?" I finally ask.

"Yeah, and when it's over you, you can't help but feel bad," she admits, and I remember how her father wants her to join the family business after school, and how her mother is completely against it.

"It's not your fault," I reply gently.

"It really is, though. I'm their only child, and dad is head of their business. Mum lets me work with him sometimes, but she still hates what he does. I'm not a fan, but I understand it's needed. It's just complicated at home," she sighs.

"What is the family business? I can't remember," I ask her.

"My dad works for the government and has his own facility, but I can't tell you what they do. It's all top secret and whatnot. I have told you this before," she laughs. I laugh it off with her because the truth is, I don't remember asking her that before. The fake past is slipping from my mind faster than I thought it was.

"I know, I thought I'd just try asking again. But seriously, it's not your fault. You can be anything you want when you finish school," I tell her.

"Not when you have to keep your parents happy, and have responsibility thrown at you from birth," she says and then shakes her head. "Anyway, less depressing talk about things we can't change, and more shopping." I smile at her, and let her lead me towards the clothes shops we usually buy from. We have a lot more in common than I ever knew. Neither of us ever really had a choice about our futures and what we get to do. Freedom was never an option for us.

I WALK UP the stairs quietly, holding three bags at my sides, and make my way into my bedroom. I put the bags on the floor by the door, shutting it, and switching on a light as I go. I turn around and jump at the sight of Elias on my window seat, smoking a cigarette out through the open window.

"What the hell are you doing in here? You have your own room!" I exclaim. Internally, I groan when I realize my plan to sneak out later and go to the woods to let my dragon out won't be happening. I feel her grumble in my mind, her annoyance isn't too bad, though.

"I said we would talk, and I meant it. I don't forget things," he says, and I mentally cringe. He *has* forgotten things, he's forgotten everything. Everything that makes him Elias Fire, the deadly dragon guard I know. I watch him finish his cigarette, flicking it out the window and shutting it before facing me. I keep my back against the wall near the door, unsure whether to approach him or not.

"What do you want me to say?" I ask, knowing I can't tell him about the real reason my eyes changed colour, or why I lied to him. I have a feeling Elias knows when I'm lying, and at the moment, I'm having to lie about everything. How I feel, what is real, what isn't, and my entire life.

"I dream about kissing you, not in a made-up dream, but an actual memory. I remember kissing you. How is that possible? We have never met, but I know you're mine. That dream fucking haunts me even when I'm awake," he tells me as he gets up and stalks over to me, never taking his eyes off mine. Every step he makes to get closer to me is dangerous, because of what I'm feeling, what I'm thinking. I don't want to lie to him, and yet, I can't let him closer. I can't tell him anything, but he doesn't remember enough to save himself. He pushes me further into the wall, his body pressed against mine. I close my eyes, knowing I can't be trusted to look at him.

"I know if I kiss you right now, you will taste as sweet as a peach and more addictive than anything I've ever tasted in my life," he growls, and I feel a finger tracing down my cheek, towards my neck. His hand slides to the back of my head, gripping my nape and angling my face towards his. Even then, I still don't open my eyes, not even when I feel his warm breath on my lips. I know he is inches away from me, and if he kisses me, I won't have the power to stop him. To fight what feels right.

"Open those eyes and tell me the truth," he urges, yet it feels like a demand. A dark, seductive one that sends shivers through me.

"I can't," I whisper, freezing when I feel his hand tighten on my neck, and his lips ever so gently brush mine.

"Soon then," he promises, and lets me go. He steps back, and I release the breath I'd been holding. I open my eyes, seeing him open the bedroom door and walk out without another word.

What the hell am I doing?

CHAPTER
EIGHT
DAGAN

"I can't stand this anymore," I yell, slamming my hand into the stone wall. Korbin looks up as he does another sit up, and then rolls back into a crouch.

"Keep it down, Elias never gets any rest. Work out, keep yourself occupied, do anything but think. It's what I do," he snaps, nodding a head towards Elias sleeping in the corner. I look into the other dungeons, seeing the other dragons in here. Most have no idea why they were taken, others have said they side with the ice throne and its true leader. Isola isn't here to save them, or to be on the throne, and she needs us.

"It's been two years! Two years of living in this cage, stuck in this dungeon, while we wait for him to bring us food!" I growl, though I quickly lose my bluster. Sighing,

I lean back against the wall and think of the only person that makes all this worth it. Isola.

"I miss her, too, and the connection makes separation painful for us all," Korbin says as he sits down next to me. I don't reply, I don't need to confirm how I'm feeling. We all know, because we're all experiencing the same emotions. When we saved her life, we didn't expect to be separated from her.

"I can't even connect to her," I growl again.

"It's because we've been weakened, and she is lost in her own mind. Connecting to her dreams is impossible," Korbin replies.

"Maybe she is better lost, because when she remembers . . . it will break her," I say quietly. She is strong, one of the strongest people I know, but none of us expected Thorne to betray her the way he did. Never expected him to kill her father, to imprison her guards, and take her throne.

"But she will have us," he comments.

"Yet, she won't. We can't escape this," I mutter back, getting angry all over again. Flames burst out of my hands, and I roll them around, forming a dragon. We are silent as I play with the flames, but eventually, I put them out and watch the door to the dungeons. Thorne should be here with food soon. He always shows up like clockwork every five days, around the same time of day.

Elias wakes up, but stays quiet as he waits for the door to open with the rest of us. The door soon opens, but instead of coming in with the usual two guards, Thorne arrives with the seer at his side. The one that made Isola forget.

"Get up," Thorne demands as he lifts his hand, showing us keys and unlocking our cage. We all stand to hurry out, but Elias is first through the open cell door. He immediately walks over and drives his fist into Thorne's face.

"What the fuck? I'm getting you out of here, you moron!" Thorne sputters, rubbing his jaw as his nose bleeds.

"That's for Isola. Don't even say you didn't deserve it," Elias says as they stare at each other. Thorne eventually nods, and turns away, walking up the stairs.

"Come on, we don't have long to get you out. Be ready to fly," he says, and we follow him out of the dungeons.

"And be ready to forget, it is the only way because I've seen all your deaths if you just go to her. Including my sister's, and I will not risk that," the seer says, just as darkness blurs everything.

"Anything for Isola, even my memories, even my dragon," are the last words I manage to hear myself say.

. . .

I WIPE my face and give myself a shake, trying to clear my mind of the dream I've had every night since we arrived. I force myself to focus on the fact I'm in class, and it's not real. I glance over at Isola, staring at the beauty sitting two rows in front of me. Like she can feel my eyes on her, she turns, and her pale-blue eyes lock with mine. Everything disappears, the classroom, the school, until there is nothing but us gazing at each other. Her blue eyes are like a pool of clear water, they suck you in until you don't want to escape. Her blonde hair is light, so natural, as it frames her face, falling in perfect waves. She is stunning and utterly irresistible, and I've only known her a few days.

"Mr. Fire? Do you know the answer?" someone asks, and reality rushes back as I realise the teacher was talking to me.

"I completely missed the question, miss, what did you say?" I ask.

"Perhaps try listening next time, Mr. Fire. I asked what made Juliet decide to kiss the poison lips of Romeo when she awoke?" she asks me. I look at Isola as I answer.

"Juliet knew she couldn't live without the one person that made life worth living. She wanted to follow Romeo anywhere, and that included death.

She made the choice that he was worth more than herself," I answer, and Isola takes a deep breath, before turning around and facing the front.

"Correct, Mr. Fire. Now can someone tell me what happened when the poison didn't work?" she asks, and Isola puts her hand up. "Go on, Miss Dragice."

"In her utter agony at the poison not working, she picked up a dagger and stabbed herself through the heart. She was certain that the only way to be with him was in death, so she guaranteed it the only way she knew how. Many people were sad and jealous of such a tragic love, that death was the only way for them to be together," she answers. The teacher claps, turning to the white board as she keeps talking. I don't hear a word of it as I watch Isola, like I have since I got to this school. There's something different about her, and there's something different about me when I'm around her, too. *I can't stay away, and I have no plan to try either.*

CHAPTER
NINE

ISOLA

I look up at the gym, the building I've avoided ever since I remembered who I was. The place where Jace died, the place that holds a memory I don't want to replay, but I need to. The final bell rings, and I square my shoulders, holding my head up as I walk in. The normal smells of socks and body odor fill my senses as I walk through the small room and into the main part of the gym. I stare at the spot where he died, seeing nothing other than a newly painted floor. Any sign Jace died here is gone, everything about him is gone from this place. Meanwhile, I'm forced to stay here and pretend everything is normal. Ignoring my teacher's shouts for me to return, I turn around and leave the building. I can't act normal in that class, in that room. It's

66

too much. I wipe my tears away as I walk out of the school and head towards the bus stop. I just want to go home and feel like shit for the rest of the evening. Everything is just so fucked up, and damn if I have a clue what I'm doing.

"Hey!" Dagan shouts, and I slow down so he can reach my side.

"Skipping class? I didn't think you had it in you, kitty cat," Dagan says as he catches up to me on my way to the bus stop.

"It's been a shit day," I tell him dryly, looking away as I can't deal with trying to get him to remember right now.

"So, I have Jules's car today as she wants me to do a food shop for her. Problem is, I have no idea how to find the supermarket," he says, grabbing my arm gently, so I stop walking. "Would you show me?"

"Why are you shopping for Jules, anyway?"

"Apparently, the three of us eat too much and keep her busy with all the extra washing we've caused. Jules is tired of constantly having to go to the shops, and told us we needed to start helping," he says, rubbing the back of his neck and making his shirt ride up. I quickly pull my eyes away, looking up at him and sighing.

"Fine. I could use some chocolate and ice cream," I reply. I follow him back to the car park, and he opens the door for me, letting me in.

"Take the main road out of town, and then it's three rights to get to the Tesco," I explain to him, as it's pretty hard to find. I don't know why they didn't just buy a building in town to put the store in, but they didn't.

"So, why are you skipping class?" Dagan asks me after he starts driving.

"Why are you?" I counter.

"I don't like gym," he explains simply, no excuse, he is just stating a fact. "You're turn."

"I don't want to talk about it."

"Come on, I want to know," he nudges my shoulder gently. Dagan catches and holds my gaze when he finds me looking at him, "I want to help, let me."

"You can't help, not with this," I mutter.

"Explain, and then we will see," he replies.

"Fine. My boyfriend died in the gym, and I went there today. I don't know, it just freaked me out, and upset me," I tell him, and he nods.

"How did he die?"

"A fire a few years ago," I say, because I can't

really tell him the truth. That my step-aunt stabbed him through the heart with a dagger.

"I'm sorry, I really am. They say you never lose someone close to you, not really. Not in here," he points at his chest.

"But you miss them. You miss them so much it hurts, sometimes," I say, and he reaches over, lifting my hand and just silently holding it.

"I can't relate to you, I can't tell you how to feel. So, I won't, but I can be here as your friend, or whatever you want me as, Isola," he says, more serious than he is ever usually like with me.

"I sometimes wonder if Jace would hate me for moving on, for even thinking of someone else that way."

"If he loved you, no, he wouldn't. He would want you to be happy, to love, and to live life to the fullest. That's all anyone wants for someone they love, and I'm sure he felt that way about you," he says, just as we spot the Tesco. We take two more turns until we pull into the car park and get out. I hadn't realized until he lets go, but he'd been holding my hand, lightly stroking it with his thumb, the entire time we'd been talking.

"Did she give you a list?" I ask, wanting to

change the subject. From the look Dagan throws me over the car bonnet, he realises, but still allows it.

"Yeah, not that I have a clue what half the things on here are," he shrugs, pulling a list out of his pocket.

"Okay, you push the trolley, and I'll put things in, nice and simple," I say, opening the list and seeing mainly herbs, meat, and fresh food. There is also, in big bold letters at the bottom saying, "Buy your own junk food."

"Apparently, you need to buy your own junk food," I show Dagan, who chuckles as he gets a trolley, and we walk into the store. It's really strange how normal this is, shopping in the human world with Dagan, a big scary dragon. I'm sure he never would have done this if he remembered who he is.

"Okay, so let's get the junk food first. It's near the entrance," I muse, and Dagan claps his hands.

"You should hold the trolley then," he grins as he starts throwing god knows how much junk food into the trolley. When it's basically full, we are at the end of the aisle.

"You can't possibly eat all this!" I say, just not believing it.

"I don't want to come back to the store, and Korbin and Elias will eat shit-loads, too," he shrugs, and then steps backwards. Everything seems to slow down, just like in the movies, as Dagan bumps into a stack of dozens of cereal boxes piled on top of each other in a triangle shape, and they go flying everywhere.

"Whoops," Dagan says, straightening up, and we look over to see an angry shop assistant glaring at us.

"Dagan," I hiss, turning the trolley around and getting the hell out of there. Dagan and I basically run down the aisle and into the next one, both of us stopping to stare at each other before bursting out laughing. By the time we stop laughing, we have tears running down our faces.

"Come on, before they find us and we get kicked out," I tease him. He takes the trolley as I get the list back out. This was just what I needed to cheer me up. Dagan is just what I needed.

"I'll go get the last bag, don't worry about it," I say, stopping Dagan from walking out of the kitchen. He chucks his keys at me, and I reach out a hand to catch them. I eye the twenty or so bags lying all over the kitchen and mentally sigh. It's going to take forever to unpack all the junk food he has bought.

"Okay, I will start putting everything away. Can you lock the car when you're finished?" he asks me, rolling that lip ring between his lips, and totally distracting me enough to drop the keys. I reach down, picking them up as I mentally curse myself. *Gotta get it together, Isola.*

"Sure," I smile at him, and walk out. The sun is bright today, making it almost warm, unlike the usual cold, wet weather we have. I walk out to the car and reach into the boot.

"*Danger,*" my dragon's voice warns me, hissing the word in my mind. I open my senses, still trying to act normal. As I'm reaching for the last bag, I hear it, the sound of something flying at me from behind. I turn, and hold both of my hands out, making an ice wall just as two daggers slam into it, one cutting my hand.

"Shit," I hiss in pain as I lower my hand, seeing the deep cut but knowing I have bigger problems. I slowly look around the ice wall, keeping my senses open, but see nothing. I can't smell anyone around either, only the residual scents of the people living with me.

"*Dragon? Can you sense them?*" I ask her, trusting her senses.

"*Gone,*" she whispers. Looking back at the wall of ice, I spin around and kick the bottom, and it falls to pieces. I reach down and pull one of the daggers out of the ice. It is dragonglass, with a red dragon symbol etched into the wooden handle. The second one is the same.

"Isola?" Dagan shouts from inside, and I quickly throw the dagger into the boot of the car. I pull the second one out, shoving that in too. I will have to remember to get these out before Jules sees them and has a heart attack. I grab the last grocery bag with my good hand, cursing at the blood dripping freely from the other, and shutting the boot. I look at the ice briefly, hoping it will melt before anyone sees it. I run up the stairs, looking behind me once more for any threats, before shutting the front door.

"What the hell happened?" Dagan says, dropping the cereal box in his hands, and rushing over to me when I get into the kitchen. He lifts my cut hand, pulling me into the kitchen, so he can see it under the spotlights, and picking up a towel, placing it on the cut.

"I, err . . . shut my hand in the boot door," I claim, the only thing I can think of, as I put the plastic food bag down on the floor.

"When you said you *try* not to be clumsy, you weren't lying, right?" he asks, a small concerned smile on his lips, making me chuckle.

"Yep," I reply, and he shakes his head at me.

"Hold this on it while I go get the first aid box," he presses my free hand on the towel and steps away.

"It's under the sink in the bathroom downstairs," I tell him. He nods, heading in that direction. I watch him walk away, as I run the image of the dagger through my mind. It wouldn't be Tatarina's or someone she sent, because I have no doubt she would use a dagger with an ice dragon and fire dragon on it to make a point when killing me. I guess it could be her, yet she would make a curse by killing me because of Bee, and she isn't that stupid. Thorne doesn't want me dead, he made that clear by stopping his mother from killing me before. *So, who would do this?* Dagan comes back, and I try to relax, attempting to forget that someone just tried to kill me. *Even though that's impossible.*

"Let's go upstairs. Jules will be home any minute, and I don't want to explain this to her. She will only freak out and want me to go to hospital," I say, hopping off the seat after Dagan nods his agreement.

"If it needs anything more than butterfly stitches, we still might have to go," Dagan says once we get to the top of stairs. When we reach my room, I open the door with my elbow.

"I heal fast, so don't worry," I reply, walking into my room. Dagan switches the light on, and I sit on the bed, moving the towel to look at the cut. It's pretty deep, straight across my tree mark, splitting the tree in half. It has begun to heal a little already, and I doubt it even needs butterfly stitches, just a bandage will do. Dagan sits next to me on the bed, pulling my hand to him, and inspecting it. He gets some antibacterial wipes out of the box and starts slowly wiping the blood away.

"I didn't know you had a tattoo," he says, admiring the tree mark. "Do you have any others?" When he slides a thumb over it, a burst of warmth shoots through me, and he quickly moves his thumb away. Dagan continues to clean my hand, though he keeps giving me strange looks.

"Nope, just this one," I answer, clearing my throat and wondering what the hell that was.

"The green ink is amazing, so unique," he comments, and I flinch as he wipes the cut, the cleaning solution burning the cut.

"Sorry, kitty cat, I should have warned you that would sting," Dagan comments, stroking my wrist with his fingers in a soothing way.

"It's okay, thanks for helping me," I reply. I close my eyes and inhale his smoky scent as he wipes the cut again, and I have to bite my lip at the sting. He smells like home, like everything I really didn't know I needed.

"Anything you need, you come to me," he commands as I open my eyes. Looking up, his blue eyes hold such promise as he stares at me. I still remember the Dagan that didn't like me, who would never look at me like this–wouldn't help me, not unless he was forced. It's still him, but he is a lot nicer, that's for sure.

"What are you thinking, kitty cat?" he asks, and I pull my eyes away from his. When I look back, he is reaching into the box for a white bandage and tape.

"I was wondering about what you like to do in your spare time?" I respond, saying the first thing I can think of.

"Other than catching you from falling, and fixing your injuries?" he jokes, making me laugh. "Well, I like to work out. The basement gym here is pretty good." I smile tightly, remembering all the times Jace and I would train and fight in that basement. How our first time was actually in there, on one of the sofas. It wasn't romantic, we were both drunk and had no idea what we were doing, but it still meant something.

"Hold still a sec," Dagan says, letting go of my hand. Putting the bandage underneath, he wraps my hand tightly before ripping some tape and tying it. This reminds me of when I cut my hands in Dragca, and Thorne fixed me up. All that time he was planning to betray me, but as I look up at Dagan, I just feel confused. Sending them to me was helping me somehow; it couldn't have been done for any other reason.

"Tell me about your childhood, your parents?" I ask Dagan, needing a change of subject, as he puts the spare stuff away. I pick up the wrappers, walking over to my bin and dropping them in. I sit on the window seat, pulling up my legs.

"My mum and dad work for the army, so there's a lot of travelling. We went everywhere, moving every month or so. It wasn't much fun moving all the time," he says each word like a robot who was programmed to say this speech. I smile tightly, wondering how far I can push his memory. I remember seeing Elias hold his head, the pain of remembering before it was time overwhelming him, I suspect. I need to push Melody into talking to me, telling me what she knows of my future and how to make them remember.

"What about you, your parents?" he asks.

"My mother and father are dead, but I have a half-sister and uncle. They just don't live around here," I say, feeling weird about talking about my sister so casually when it still feels so raw.

"Jules said she talks to your father, and he pays her?" he asks me, his suspicious eyes narrowing on mine.

"She means my uncle, he claims to be my father sometimes," I lie, and I know he knows it when he tuts.

"You're not a good liar, you should work on that, kitty cat," he says and picks the first aid box up, walking to the door. He stops when he opens it, looking back at me.

"When you came back in that kitchen, you were scared. Is it safe for me to leave you?"

"Of course, it is," I say, trying to wave it off.

"If you need a guard, a friend, or *anything* . . . I'm only two doors away," he says and walks out, the look in his eyes staying with me. He knows I'm hiding something. Even when he doesn't remember who he is, or who I am, he still wants to guard me. For some reason, it makes my heart flutter.

CHAPTER
ELEVEN
ISOLA

I shoot my eyes open, seeing a gun pointing at another version of me. My hair is up in a pony-tail, and I have my dragon leather outfit on, which gives me hope that I get back to Dragca at some point. I can't see who is holding the gun, only the slight wobble of the person's hand as they hold it in front of my face. I don't move, just hold my hands up, and speak words I can't hear. I can't even see the room, only a smoky blur instead.

"Hey, sis!" I hear Melody say cheerfully, making me jump. Why do people keep appearing out of nowhere? I turn to see her walk through the smoke, wearing the same red dress as last time I saw her. Her hair is up in a bun this time, and her marks on her face almost glow in the dimly lit room.

"Another warning vision?" I ask.

"Oh this, no . . . well, yes. It doesn't matter, I only use them to be able to talk to you, as the visions won't change," she waves a hand like someone holding my future self at gunpoint isn't important.

"Someone tried to kill me, with daggers," I tell her, and she sighs.

"Thorne thinks he controls his mother, that she isn't stupid enough to kill you. He doesn't know her at all. Watch your back," she warns me.

"I wish people would stop coming into my dreams, it's just annoying now," I give her a pointed look, but she just raises an eyebrow at me.

"And I wish I didn't have to use my power every day to keep you safe, but we all don't get what we want. Now grow up, get over it, and listen," she tells me off, and surprised, I decide to listen. She does have a point.

"What is going on in Dragca? Has anyone seen my uncle?" I ask, needing to know what is going on. He is all I have left who is on my side over there, that I know of anyway. If I can get to him, then I can figure something out. I don't think walking back into Dragca with no plan is a good idea. I remember how Tatarina looked at me; she wants me dead, and I have a feeling Bee and the curse is the only reason I'm not.

"No, we haven't found him, but that's a good thing.

He is hiding with the seers, somehow; smart man," she pauses to wink. "Anyway, your stepbrother is being ruled by his mother. She is an evil bitch, just in case you were unsure, and his dear auntie is her executioner. The whole of Dragca is split with those who are scared but secretly hope you are still alive, and those who support Thorne but are scared of his mother. Then there are others who don't know who to choose, so they are going to the seers, who will not choose a side anymore," she explains.

"I will come back soon and convince the seers to side with me. With you by my side, it shouldn't be too difficult," I promise.

"Oh, I know, only . . . it's not going to be as easy as you think. Once you come back, I'm not seeing all your future, just bits, like this gunshot . . . it's bothering me. I see you coming for me, and then it's black. I'm missing something," she says, frustration written all over her face.

"Can I stop Thorne from coming into my dreams? Is there any way you can tell me how to make the guys remember?" I ask her, knowing this dream can't last forever, and talking about the future isn't what I need to know.

"No, it's fate, and good for you both," she says, with a sad smile. She looks over her shoulder at something, but I *only see smoke. When she looks back, the sad smile is replaced with tight lines.*

"Which is?" I ask.

"All of this, it's what has to happen, and there are so many outcomes that could occur. I could tell you the clearest route, but then it would risk that future. First rule of being a seer, you don't tell your closest family their futures, unless you want them dead," she says, seeming happy, and then she looks behind herself again. Her smile disappears, and worry fills her face instead.

"What are you looking at?" I ask.

"I'm projecting from my room while half-asleep, and Thorne is knocking on the door," she says and turns back. "I don't have much time as he wants me to look for you again, tell him what you are doing, and that means his mother is out for a bit," she explains.

"I hate him, Odie! I can't and don't want to see him in my dreams. Also, I don't want you telling him what I'm doing!" I shout at her.

"Have you ever heard the saying 'there's a fine line between love and hate'?" she asks, but a gunshot makes me jump before I can yell at her about her ridiculous idea. I don't love Thorne, I detest him. I can't stand him for what he has done. I look over to see the future me holding my stomach, the person with the gun actually

shot me. Who is it? I try to walk over, but something stops me, like a glass wall I can't see.

"Time to wake up, your dragon guards need you, and time is short," Melody tells me. I go to correct her about the love and hate thing, and the stupid saying which is bugging me when I know there are more important things to find out. Like who shot me.

"I've been shot, who is that?" I bite out.

"Oh, that's nothing, and you know I can't tell you. I know you live . . . if that helps," she chuckles, and then everything blurs away. Being shot isn't nothing, but I don't get to tell her that.

THE SHRIEKING of my alarm makes me wake up. I'm feeling a little hazy as I rub my eyes and grab my phone. The memory of the dream flashes through my mind. I'm going to be shot in the future, which I bet really hurts. Why didn't I defend myself, fight them? It doesn't make any sense. I don't even want to think about that knowing look my sister gave me, like I could love Thorne. That's impossible, so fucking impossible. I turn the alarm off, scrolling blankly through my Facebook messages from Hallie. I guess she went on a date last night with some guy, and apparently, he's really good in bed. *At least someone is getting laid.* I think I'm starting to forget what sex is like. I send her a quick text about how lucky she is, and then start to get out of bed, when someone knocks on my door. I run over, open it up, and keep myself behind the door as my banana-covered pajamas aren't cute. Neither are the Dorito stains all over them.

"I can't run this morning, I have to go and look at a car that's for sale across town. Elias is coming with me, and Jules as well, because she just wants to get out of the house," Korbin says. I nod as I run my eyes over his styled brown hair, green eyes, and the tight shirt and jeans he has on. They cling to his body, showing off how damn impressive it is.

"It's Saturday anyway, I don't run on weekends," I make myself look away as I reply.

"Cool, that works out then. Be ready at seven tonight," he instructs, stepping back.

"Seven?" I ask.

"I'm a little insulted you forgot about our date, doll, but you can make it up to me tonight," he says with a wink. I mentally sigh as he turns around and walks away. We can't date, it's too risky for them, for me. Yet, somehow the thought of going out on a date with Korbin turns me on much more than it frightens me. I shut the door, mentally cursing myself, and try to decide whether or not letting my hormones control me is the best idea. I pull the bandage off my hand and, despite the cut being healed, get a plaster out to replace it. I should have something covering where the cut should be, just in case Dagan sees it. I get changed and grab my Kindle, intent on spending the day reading a romantic wolf-shifter book. Running down the stairs, I freeze when I see Dagan in the kitchen, cooking something that smells amazing. He even has an apron on, no shirt underneath, and I just stare at all the muscles on his back. There are a few scars littered around, but mainly it is all muscles, and damn fine-looking ones at that.

"I didn't have you down as the cooking type," I grin, and he turns to look at me.

"Oh, and what did you have me down as?" he teases.

"A guy that lifts weights all day and likes to fight," I shrug, as really, he does seem like that type, and back in Dragca, there was no need for him to cook at the academy.

"I do fight, so you're right there. In fact, I have a self-defence class today that I'm going to for the first time," he chuckles and then looks over at me as he pours batter into the frying pan.

"Want some pancakes?" he asks.

"I'd love some," I reply, walking over to the table. Dagan serves the pancakes up before sitting opposite me. After pouring some maple syrup on the pancakes, we begin eating in earnest, not really speaking. Every so often, I feel his eyes on me, but whenever I glance up, he is looking away and pretending like he wasn't. I need to do something to get some alone time with him, where we have a chance to talk, and he isn't so awkward with me.

"How's your hand?" he asks, reminding me that I need to get the daggers out of the car before Jules sees them.

"Fine," I respond, and he nods.

"Can I come to self-defence? I used to go to the local one a few years back," I blurt out.

"Really? You did self-defence?" he asks, leaning back in his chair, and looking me up and down. *Why do guys think females can't fight simply because we don't look strong?* Usually, the strongest people in the world are hidden behind a pretty face.

"Yes, I did, and I bet I can kick your ass," I say, totally bluffing. Dagan is like twice the size of me, and most likely could break me like a twig.

"I'd like to see that, but you hurt your hand. It's not a good idea."

"It's all healed, I swear I'm fine," I say, and he narrows his eyes at me.

"Alright then. We have Elias's bike we can ride there, as he took the taxi with Korbin and Jules earlier," he tells me.

"I will clean up, you cooked," I say when we have finished eating, but Dagan picks his plate up and moves to get mine.

"Nah, I don't mind, and you need to get dressed. Class starts in an hour, and we'll need to leave in ten minutes to get there," he explains.

"Okay," I say, getting up and keeping my eyes on him. "A hot man that cooks and cleans, most girls would do anything to find a guy like you." I instantly regret it when I realise I said it out loud.

"You think I'm hot?" Dagan teases, as my cheeks light up.

"That was meant to be a comment in my head, not spoken out loud," I explain, which only makes his grin grow. He rolls the lip ring in-between his lips and puts the plates down, walking over to me. He stops when we are mere inches apart, and I have to arch my neck to look up at him.

"Go and get dressed before I show you just how *hot* I think you are, kitty cat," he warns me, and yet, I don't move as I stare up at him. His blue eyes are brighter now, the black specks from his dragon are gone, and I kind of miss them.

"What are you thinking about?" he asks me, his voice deep and husky as he strokes his fingers down my arm. His touch snaps me out of my thoughts and brings me back to my senses. I step back, clearing my throat.

"About how a girl is going to beat your ass in class," I say with a grin, and turn away before I do something crazy, like jump on him and kiss him until we both forget everything else.

CHAPTER
TWELVE
ISOLA

"Ouch," I groan as Dagan flips me onto my back, and I wheeze out in pain. He looks down at me, his hands on his hips, and his dark eyebrows raised. I huff mentally, knowing I'm not using all my strength, because to do that would be to call my dragon for help. I have to put a large barrier between us, just so she doesn't take offence at Dagan's smirk every damn time he wins. *Cocky asshole.*

"How long has it been since you trained?" he asks, offering me a hand which I push away and get myself up. There are a few other people training, and they look our way, but they don't stare for long. Most of the humans are scared of Dagan, and have been since we walked in, which works well to get them to leave us alone. The training hall is right in the middle of town, at the back of a warehouse. The place is used for all sorts of sports, I believe; the stench of sweat, dirt, and blood is overwhelming me.

"Months, years, I don't know," I manage to pant out. Dagan rolls his lip ring as he watches me. All I can think about is how I want to kiss him, want to feel that cold silver of the ring against my own lips. I shouldn't be thinking these things.

"You need a lot of work before you would stand a chance of beating *anyone*," he says, and the teacher chooses that point to walk over.

"Isola had a lot of skill from what I remember; with some personal training she could be a worthy opponent in a fight," Miss Dale says, smiling. Miss Dale is thirty-something with bright-pink hair cut very short, and a muscular, toned body that most people would die for. She also has a serious expression that makes you want to run away from her. She is tiny, like five-foot-three, but she could kick all our asses without even getting breathless. Well, maybe not Dagan, but then he has trained all his life, even if he doesn't remember it.

"I don't see any skill now," Dagan comments drily, like I'm not right in front of him.

"Maybe you should give her some lessons. The skills on your paperwork indicate you don't really need this class anyway, so why not train someone in need, instead?" Miss Dale suggests.

"I'm not in need," I protest.

"You are, and being the good person I am, I will help you," Dagan cockily replies, and I just glare at him as Miss Dale claps.

"Excellent," she says with a sweet smile towards me. "Why don't you get the Bo staff and fight with those? I remember you being amazing with one," she suggests, nodding her head towards the large fighting ring in the middle of the hall. The Bo staffs are lined up next to it. It's a common way to fight here, and I used to be able to beat everyone other than Jace. He was something else as a fighter, but everyone has forgotten him here. This is a place he came to every week, and they can't remember him. I close my eyes, looking away for just a second to calm down from the rush of anger that makes me feel.

"Okay," Dagan says, walking over to the ring, and I follow reluctantly. This is going to hurt both my ego and my butt when he beats me. I grab a Bo staff from the rack, and climb into the ring after Dagan. He stands, swirling the Bo staff around with one hand as he watches me from the other side of the ring.

"This might hurt a little, but I promise to be gentle," he comments, and runs at me before I'm ready to even reply. I lift my staff, whacking it against his and spinning around straight after, meeting his next hit. Dagan jumps to the left, swinging the staff for my legs, which I manage to avoid with a backflip. I land with my staff up, ready to protect myself, as he attacks again. He pushes all his strength down onto me, and I have to take several steps back, keeping my eyes locked onto his blue ones.

"Is that what you tell all the girls? That you will be gentle?" I tease him, trying to distract him enough to escape the corner I'm backed in.

"Wouldn't you like to know what I tell them," he answers, just as my back hits the ring's barrier.

"Not if that's what you tell them. I don't like *gentle*," I say, biting my lip, and he pauses. That moment of hesitation is all I need to push him back. I sweep my staff under his legs, and he lands hard on the floor, on his back. I place the end of my staff against his neck before he can even blink.

"Kitty cat, I'm impressed," he coughs out.

"You haven't seen anything yet," I laugh, moving

the staff and straightening up. "Again." I grin at his shocked smile.

"I think I'm going to like you, kitty cat," he says. He jumps up, slamming his staff into mine with the slight distraction his words cause, and all I can do is laugh.

"Will I be seeing you here next week?" Miss Dale asks me as I come out of the changing rooms.

"Yes, I think I will be coming every week for a while," I reply, and she smiles, placing her hand on my arm.

"Does that have anything to do with a certain dark-haired hottie?" she asks, and I chuckle.

"Dagan? No, it's not like that with us," I deny.

"No one looks at each other the way you two do without there being something between them," she squeezes my arm once and walks away. Standing still, I roll her words around my mind as I watch her walk out of the hall. I want to deny it all, say she is wrong, and there's nothing between us . . . but I hate lying, especially to myself. I just have to keep my distance from him and the others. I can't risk it all, not just for my feelings. Not when there's a curse that could take everything from me, from them. I watch Dagan walk out of the male changing room, chatting to some guy who pats his shoulder like they are friends. Dagan looks around for me, a small smile playing on his lips when he spots me. He says something to the guy, who looks over at me, and then smirks at Dagan before walking off. Dagan walks over to me, his eyes staying locked on mine like there isn't anyone else in the room. The moment is so intense and breathtaking that it's hard to control my own desires and continue to try to convince myself there's nothing between us.

"Kitty cat, let's go and get some lunch. Where is best to eat around here?" Dagan asks me.

"There's a deli two doors away, they do amazing sandwiches," I say. "They have these peanut butter bacon sandwiches which are my favourite."

"Peanut butter and bacon in a sandwich? That sounds gross," he shakes his head at me.

"Don't knock it until you try it," I say, making him laugh as he opens the gym doors for me. I walk out, and he immediately follows.

"It looks like it might rain, we should hurry up," he says, and I look up, seeing the dark-grey clouds and feeling the chill in the air. He is right. We rush around the corner, but we're too late as the skies open up, and rain pounds down on us. I see the deli not far from us, its purple door is easy to spot.

"Shit, run, it's not far," I say, grabbing Dagan's hand and running down the street to the deli. I pull the door open and rush inside, trying to catch my breath.

"We are both soaked," Dagan comments. Something in his tone has me looking down at my white shirt and yoga pants. A blush rises up my cheeks when I notice my shirt is see-through, and you can see my pink bra underneath. I look up, seeing Dagan's eyes drift over my body, and then back up to my eyes. There's a moment where we stare at each other, and I'm sure we are thinking and feeling the same things, but neither of us move. We just stare, until he decides to step forward, leaving us only a breath apart. Just as he reaches forward to touch me, a voice interrupts.

"I got you some towels, the weather is awful this time of year," a sweet, older-sounding voice says. I turn to look at the lady speaking to us. She is about fifty, with hair dyed purple and cut short, and a big smile on her lips as she looks between us, holding out some white towels.

"Thank you, it just came down so quick," I say,

accepting one of the towels and stepping back from Dagan.

"Why don't you sit over here, the heater is under the table, so it will dry you off," she points to a small table for two by the wall.

"Thanks, can we have two peanut butter bacon sandwiches and some teas, please?" I ask, seeing Dagan glare at me from the corner of my eye.

"Perfect, I will get right on that," she says, writing the order down on a notepad and walking off.

"I'm not eating that," Dagan says as we walk over to the table.

"Come on, you have to try it. Fair enough if you don't like it, but trying new things is fun," I say, and he shakes his head at me as he slides into his seat opposite mine. I glance around seeing the empty deli, and out the window where it is still pounding down with rain. Thank god Dagan parked the bike in the car park opposite the gym, so it won't be wet when we get to it.

"I'm not leaving here until that stops," I say, and Dagan looks at the rain outside briefly before turning back to me.

"It's likely just a shower, and will be over soon," he says. The lady brings our drinks and food over a few minutes later, placing them onto the table. I practically drool at the sight of my favourite sandwich. It's been so long since I've had one of these. I pick it up, taking one big bite, trying not to moan out loud at the amazing taste.

"I know what to buy you if I piss you off," he comments, making me chuckle.

"When, *when* you piss me off. Now man up and try yours," I nod my head at his plate. He narrows his eyes at me as he picks the sandwich up. He sniffs it before taking a bite, and I watch like it's almost in slow motion.

"Soooo?" I ask as he puts the sandwich down.

"It's okay," he says, and I laugh.

"You like it! You just won't admit that I'm right," I say, raising an eyebrow.

"I have no idea what you are talking about," he says with a grin and picks up his sandwich. He takes a big bite, and I try not to laugh. *Stubborn dragon.*

THIRTEEN

ISOLA

"This is a bad idea, such a bad idea, Issy," I say to myself, smoothing down the tight red dress. Pushing my curly hair over my shoulder, I stare at myself in the mirror. I glance at the clock on the wall, seeing it's nearly seven and time for my date with Korbin. I'm kind of hoping the red dress I bought will jog his memory of the mating ceremony. I'm running out of ideas on how to make the guys remember me, and that's not good. The more time I spend away from Dragca, the more I have no idea what's going on. I keep thinking about the seers, wondering how I'm going to convince them that fighting for me and protecting me is a good idea. How I'm going to convince anyone to help me get the throne back. I still jump a

99

little when a knock sounds at my door, even though I'm expecting it. I walk over, picking up my leather jacket hanging on the back of the door before opening it.

"Wow," Korbin mutters as I just stare at him, speechless at how amazing he looks. Korbin's hair is styled a little, making his eyes pop, and he's wearing a blue shirt, black trousers, with a long black coat.

"Oh, snap," I say, and then shake my head as my cheeks burn. "That was really lame. You look good, is what I meant to say," I blurt out. He laughs, stepping closer.

"You're cute when you're nervous, Issy," he tells me, and I chuckle.

"Cute and weird, you sure you want to take me out?" I ask.

"Certain," he grins seductively.

"So . . . where are we going?" I ask, as he hasn't told me a thing about this date. Korbin clears his throat, holding his hand out for me. I slide my hand into his, feeling the roughness of it from his training, I expect.

"It's a ten-minute drive, and no, I'm not telling you where we are going as it's a surprise," he says, leading me down the corridor, and still holding my hand. We're walking to the door, when someone clears their throat, and I turn around to see Dagan leaning against the wall. His eyes drift down my dress, and feel like they are burning my skin with every part they touch until he looks up.

"Have a good night," he says gruffly, his hands tensely held in fists at his sides. We trained all day, and something seems to have changed between us. Like it has been changing with Elias, like it's changing with Korbin. I don't see them as just friends, and when I'm with them, I forget the curse. I forget who I am and wish we were just normal people who could be together without any danger.

"We will," Korbin answers when I don't speak, opening the front door.

"Bye, Dagan," I say, and he nods tensely before I turn around and walk outside. It's lit up by the solar lights attached to the house and the ones running down the sides of the driveway. Parked up is a black car, which Korbin unlocks with his keys.

"It's a Vauxhall Antara, we got it today. What do you think?" he asks.

"That I'm clueless about cars, but it's nice?" I say, making him laugh as he opens my door for me. I get in, and he shuts the door as I pull my seatbelt on and wait for him to get in and do the same.

"Are you really not going to tell me what you

have planned?" I ask him, and he winks at me as he starts the car.

"Don't you trust me, doll?"

"Fine," I pout, rolling my eyes at him, and making him laugh. Korbin turns the radio on, and to my surprise, starts singing along with the lyrics of the Taylor Swift song.

"*Look what you've made me do*," he sings as I just sit watching him with wide eyes.

"What?" he asks, finally noticing me.

"I didn't have you for a Tay-Tay fan," I grin as he shrugs.

"I like to sing, it's meant to be good for you. You should try it," he suggests teasingly. I like this playful side of him, he is usually so serious and grumpy. Well, not as grumpy as Eli and Dagan, but still.

"I don't sing, and the world can thank me for that one at any time," I say, making him laugh.

"Come on, I won't tell," he winks, and I chuckle, still not singing with him. He just carries on singing like nothing happened, without a care in the world. I gently start humming along after a while, and he reaches over, taking my hand in his for the rest of the drive. I know it's only holding my hand, but it sends little warm feelings straight through to my heart. Feelings that I need to ignore in order to get through tonight. I can't really date him. It's just hard to remember that when Korbin is like this with me, winning me over with every damn look from his deep, sexy green eyes.

"Here we are," he pulls up to the beach port, a place I've never really been in all my years of living here. I give him a questioning look as we get out of the car, and walk down the pier. When the dock with five large yachts tied up comes into view, and one that is lit up with a man waiting at the end, I have a good idea what the date is.

"A yacht date?" I ask, and he nods, looking nervous.

"I love it, I haven't actually been on one before," I say, and he looks relieved as he lifts our joined hands, gently kissing my knuckles. I end up blushing at the sweet movement. *Damn, this night is going to be harder than I thought.*

"I've rented it for the night," he explains as we near the human waiting by the walkway to the yacht. The human has a suit on, dark hair, and a serious expression.

"Mr. Dragoali and Miss Dragice, I presume?" he asks, and Korbin offers him a hand to shake.

"Lovely to meet you, Mr. Gregory," he says.

G. BAILEY

"Come on board, I will be steering my yacht for the night, but you won't see me, you have it all to yourselves. So lovely to see such a happy young couple," he comments, and we walk up the ramp. Korbin slides an arm around my waist.

"One more thing, the music speakers are playing up. They might turn on and off, but let me know if it becomes a problem, and I will switch them off altogether," he tells us.

"Thank you, Mr. Gregory," I reply.

"Let's look around, I've only seen the photos online," Korbin says as we continue on. I nod, resting my head on his shoulder as we walk around. The yacht has an entire glass level, with three sofas, a bar, and other normal things spread around. It's all shiny, new, and stunning. There are doors that lead outside to the front of the yacht, where you can look over the ocean. Korbin walks down a set of stairs, and I follow, my mouth dropping open at the room below. The entire bottom of the room is glass, so you can see underneath with the bright lights in the four corners of the room. There's a table, with bowls of covered-up food on it, but I barely notice as the yacht moves.

"This is incredible," I say, moving around the room as we begin to see fish swimming below the glass. Korbin lies down on the floor, looking down, and I chuckle before lying next to him. *It's a good idea, really.*

"It's kind of like you're floating through the water," I say, "it's so beautiful," I whisper, and look over to see Korbin staring at me.

"So are you," he says, reaching for my hand, and linking our fingers together. We don't say much more as we watch the fish and the sea for a long time, until the yacht slows down. Every time I point something out, Korbin is never looking, his eyes are always on me instead. I don't know why, but the idea that I'm more fascinating than the beautiful sight in front of me is scary. Not scary because of him, but because what is happening between us isn't just nothing. It's something special, and something like this could break the curse and I don't know if that is something I want to happen while we are on earth.

"We should eat," Korbin suggests, jumping up in one smooth, sexy movement, and holding a hand out for me. I grab his hand, getting up as I clear my throat.

"It's hot in here," I comment, taking off my leather jacket. It doesn't really help, as it's not the temperature, but rather Korbin that's making me hot. Korbin takes his coat off at the same time as I do, watching me for something. It's almost like he knows what I'm thinking, but he doesn't call me out on it like he could do.

"Here," he takes mine from me, and goes to hang them on a hook near the staircase. I lift the lids on some of the plates, seeing a range of sea food, and a chocolate dessert that makes my mouth water from just one glance. I sit down as Korbin gets back to the table.

"I hope you like seafood, I should have asked before we came," he says as he takes his seat on the other side of the table.

"I love seafood. Jace couldn't stand the smell of it, so I didn't have it often," I say, mentally laughing at the scrunched-up face he used to make when it was anywhere near him. *I miss him, but his memory seems to drift further away every day.*

"Who is Jace?" Korbin asks as he picks up his knife and fork to begin eating.

"My ex-boyfriend, he died a few years ago," I say, even though it feels like it was just yesterday that I found him dead.

"I'm sorry, I truly am," he says, reaching across to hold my hand.

"I can't eat with one hand, you know?" I tease

him, trying to lighten the mood a little, and needing the subject change. It's not that I don't want to talk about Jace with him, but just not this Korbin who can't really understand my anger or need for revenge. And it would all be a lie, I can't tell him how he died, and I don't want to lie to him any more than I must. It doesn't feel right.

"Yes, you can, watch," he grins and throws a chip in the air, catching it perfectly with his mouth.

"Not all of us are that good. If I tried that, I'd end up poking my eye out with the chip and we would be in A&E," I say, and he laughs, letting go of my hand. We eat our food, occasionally commenting on how amazing it all tastes, though I still try to keep my eyes away from him as much as possible. This date is feeling too real, too much. Some slow, romantic music starts playing just as we finish, making Korbin laugh.

"So, the music is working again, and perfect timing. Would you like to dance?" he asks.

"I don't know," I mumble and he gets up, holding a hand out for me. I can't really say no when he looks at me like that, despite how dangerous this is. I place my hand in his, and get out of the seat, walking away from the table a little. Korbin pulls me close to him, with hands on my waist, and I slide my arms around his neck as I look up.

"I had this dream, that I was watching you dance, in a red dress, with someone else. All I wanted was to dance with you, hold you, but I couldn't for some reason. That dream keeps running through my mind, almost as much as your blue eyes do," he admits, making my heart pound. He is dreaming about the night I danced with Thorne at the mating ceremony, meaning he is starting to remember something. I wonder if any of the others are having dreams.

"Some people say dreams are our deepest wishes, that they could even be true," I reply, and he chuckles, taking my hand and spinning me around, before pulling me back to him.

"I don't know about wishes, but desires, yes. Dreams are definitely our deepest desires," he says, leaving me breathless as I can't look away from him. Korbin leans down, taking my lips with his when I'm not expecting it. But I can't stop the reaction I have the moment our lips meet. The kiss is deep, passionate, and perfect. Groaning when I pull him closer, Korbin lifts me up by my ass, and I lock my legs around him.

"Kor," I moan, when he kisses down my jaw,

getting to my neck and sucking, making me want him so much.

"Isola," he whispers, pulling back, his thumbs rubbing circles on my ass where he holds me to him. I slide my hands into his hair, and any hesitation he had is gone as he slams his lips into mine, lowering us to the floor. I should tell him to stop as he pushes my dress up around my waist, but I can't, I don't want to stop. Pulling the top of my dress and bra down, Korbin exposes my breast and flicks his tongue over my nipple. I moan, and in response his hand drags my underwear down my legs slowly, until I can kick them off. He slides his hand up my leg ever so slowly, teasing me as he leaves my breast to kiss me again.

"Doll, stop me," he almost begs.

"I can't, and I'm on protection. I don't want to stop," I breathe out, not lying about protection exactly, but female dragons can't get pregnant unless they are in heat, and that only happens once a year.

"Doll," his deep gravelly voice whispers next to my ear as he slips a finger inside me. I moan just as he moves his hand, each movement getting me so close to the edge.

"Damn . . . you're tight," he groans, moving his

finger out of me and making me miss it already. I hear him undo his trousers, the sound of his zipper coming down making me desperate for him as I lie down on the floor, and he follows after me. I don't have to wait long as Korbin moves his body over mine, sliding inside me with one long stroke. I feel a slight coldness of a piercing I can feel on him, shocking me a little, but it's so pleasurable that I don't care after a second. He looks down at me, buried inside me, and pushes a hand into my hair.

"Mine," he growls, and his eyes turn completely black, his dragon taking over. I moan as he starts slamming into me harder and faster.

"Mine," I moan back, my dragon agreeing with me as Korbin picks up speed with my words. I push him over onto his back, seeing his surprised look, and knowing he let me take control. I grab his shoulders as I ride him, his fingers gripping my hips tightly as I drive myself to the brink.

"I'm close, Kor," I moan out, my words barely making any sense. Kor sits up, taking my nipple into his mouth and flicking it with his tongue, and that's all I need. I come hard, and a few thrusts later, he finishes inside me, grabbing my hips hard as he bites down on my shoulder.

"Damn, I didn't expect it to be like this," he

pants out, and I kiss his cheek, as he turns to look at me.

"Do you remember?" I ask, hoping that the black I saw in his eyes means he does, but the confused look he gives me proves he doesn't.

"Remember what?" he asks.

"Nothing," I say, kissing him before he can read my expression, letting his kisses erase any disappointment that he doesn't remember, and I let myself get lost in him. We stay like that a while longer, as I try to forget the fear that when he *does* remember, he'll hate me for not stopping this because of the curse. I couldn't stand him hating me, and it makes me sick to think he might. What have I done? *When did my life get so complicated?*

FOURTEEN

Black shadows surround me, pressing against every part of my body as I try not to scream out from the pain. The bitch won't hear me scream, that's for sure. My dragon beats against my mind, but I can't let him out, the fucking seer has locked him away. I imagine Isola as the pain floods every part of me, remembering what she looks like, how sweet her lips taste. How she is mine, and once I get out of here, I will tell her that. Even if she doesn't want me, even if the curse takes everything, I will be at her side. Friend, protector, guard, or lover. It doesn't matter, I just want to see her.

"Enough, stop this!" I hear someone demand, but they won't be able to stop her, no one can.

"I said no more!" the man shouts, a growl reverber-

ating with his words this time. The black shadows move away, dropping me onto the floor. I cough blood out, wiping my mouth as I look around for Dagan and Korbin. I finally find them both passed out on the floor. The bitch started with them before me, and they couldn't handle it for too long, not that I'm far from passing out myself.

"We should kill them, they will only try to escape and help Isola. They aren't loyal to you, my son," I hear Tatarina say in her overly sweet voice. I turn to see Thorne watching me as he stands next to his mother.

"I don't want them dead, I want them available to use against her. Think about it, mother, if Isola ever remembers, or anyone tries to help her, we need someone to use against her," he explains, and I push myself up.

"You betraying bastard," I spit out, but he ignores me, still watching his mother. She pushes her pale-blonde hair over her shoulder, and I see the black veins crawling all up her arms. If it wasn't for the darkness around her, she would look so sweet and innocent with her big doll-like eyes and features. She is using a lot of dark magic, so she must have a dark spirit, the very opposite to Isola. That makes Isola her biggest threat, yet, she isn't dead. I would know if anyone killed Isola, it would destroy my soul.

"Fine, fine. We will keep them alive . . . for now. Let

them starve, no one helps them," she says and walks away. Thorne watches until she shuts the dungeon door behind her, and finally meets my eyes.

"How could you? You know what she is to you, what she could be," I growl.

"Don't, I don't need advice from you," Thorne spits out, anger burning in his eyes as his dragon turns them silver. Thorne shakes his head and reaches into his cloak, pulling out three little bottles. He puts them on the floor just inside the cage.

"Drink these, they will heal you and the others," he says, confusing me.

"Why do you care? You have your throne and everything you wanted," I ask.

"I don't care, but Isola does. For that, I will keep you alive and help you escape when the time is right," he says, and I step back, not understanding why.

"Are you going to let us go, only to use us against her somehow?" I ask. "I can't believe you would just to help her."

"Does it matter why?" he replies, but I know it's a lie, I can see it in his eyes. I don't question him on it, knowing I'm missing something. And I need to figure it out, I need to figure Thorne out.

. . .

"FUCKING HELL," I mutter, sitting up in bed as another one of those messed up dreams bothers me again. *Haunt me.* Ever since I came to this town, I can't stop dreaming of dragons, of a beautiful girl with blue eyes so clear they almost look like you can fall into them. I dream of a castle, of being locked away for years, and a guy named Thorne bringing me food–looking after me and the others. For some reason, I hate that bastard, and I want to punch him. Then there are dreams of a girl in a red dress, dancing, and looking so happy, so free. It's always Isola, but it's like she is someone else in these dreams. A princess, and a forbidden one at that. It's a total mind fuck that makes me want her more than anything. I slide out of bed, leaving my room in only my pajama shorts and walking down the corridor, pausing outside Isola's room. I've always been able to smell people, which I know isn't normal, but it's not like I can turn it off. I can smell her, mixed with the scent of Korbin. *So, their date went well, I guess. For fuck's sake.* I run down the stairs, taking the right through the lounge, and heading to the stairs that lead to the basement. I walk straight to the punching bag, lifting my hand and slamming it into it. I pour all my frustration, my hate, and my confusion into every punch, closing my eyes and shutting the world off until my hands burn.

"Eli!" I hear shouted, and I stop. Breathing heavily, I turn to see Korbin standing a few feet away from me. His hair is messy, and he's just wearing his pajama shorts, smelling so much like Isola that I want to hit him.

"You're bleeding," he points out.

"I heal quick, always have. Don't worry about it," I say, and he offers me a towel. I place it on my hands and quickly step away from him.

"How was your date?" I ask tensely, and he picks up on it.

"Good. She is mine now, Elias," he states, the possession in his voice isn't hard to pick up on. He has another thing coming if he thinks I will just walk away.

"For now, I'm not backing off. The naughty princess isn't something I'm willing to give up on," I warn him, and he walks over, until he is standing straight in front of me.

"Back off," he bites out.

"Make me," I say, being deadly serious.

"What the fuck is going on?" Dagan shouts, being the voice of reason like he usually is between us. He comes over, pushing his way in the middle of us, and I try to calm myself down. I don't really want to fight with Korbin or Dagan, yet it's hard to think of anything else right now.

"What the fuck is going on with you two idiots? Explain," he demands.

"I'm not sharing Isola, and fuck-face doesn't get that," Korbin replies in a dry tone.

"I'm guessing your date went well then?" Dagan says, and I hear the growl in his voice, making me smirk.

"You like her, too," I state, but he doesn't answer or look at me. There's a tense moment between all of us, none of us saying a word. We can't, or won't, give up on her. That means there is only one way we can have a happy ending with Isola. I think she means more to us than just some random girl. It's been more than that for me since I first saw her. I don't need them to tell me how they feel, I can see it in how they watch her.

"Yeah, you could say that," Dagan finally replies.

"Right, well, shouldn't this be Isola's decision? If she isn't interested in anyone else, you have nothing to worry about. Though, I will warn you of something, Kor," I say, stepping away from them both.

"What?" Korbin snaps.

"Isola is stubborn and smart, and I doubt you

telling her what to do will go over well," I say, and he shakes his head, looking up at the ceiling. He knows I'm right, this has to be her decision.

"She can't date us all," Korbin finally points out what we have all been skirting around.

"Why not?" I'm the only one brave enough to point that out. They just stare, in complete shock, as I walk out of the room. *Sharing or not, I can't stay away from Isola Dragice, and I won't even try.*

FIFTEEN

ISOLA

I don't need to open my eyes, I can sense him here as soon as I feel the smoke blowing around my body. I can feel him near me, I can smell his smoky scent as it surrounds me. Like it's trying to slowly choke me to death with its seductive smell. My dragon is practically purring in my mind, wanting to be closer to the man I hate.

"Issy," he says, and I finally look. Thorne is standing close to me, about a footstep away, with his hands held behind his back. His cloak moves in the breeze, swaying around the guard uniform he is wearing. The leather is stretched tightly across his chest, and when I look up, I see his blue eyes gazing at me with a look I don't understand. He isn't smiling, or frowning, just standing like a statue. Like a predator waiting for its prey to run or face *him. I hate that he looks good, so attractive to me, and I pull my eyes away from him.*

"Thorne, you don't get to call me that. It's Princess Isola to you," I reply coldly.

"I will never call you that, you will always be Issy to me," he says, stepping closer. I keep very still as he reaches a hand out to touch my hair. He tucks a stray piece behind my ear, and my heart pounds against my chest as I stare into his blue eyes. I actually wouldn't even describe them as blue, more silver than anything else. They are like silver pools, mixed with blue dots and darkness around the corners. The silver blue colour bounces off his blonde hair, which only serves to remind me of who he is.

"I hate you," is all I can think to say, and then I move away, clearing my throat. Telling him I hate him has become a defence mechanism, because I can't say anything else. I can't feel anything else.

"I deserve for you to hate me, I don't expect anything less," he says, his words hollow as I hear the pain in them.

"Why? Why are the guys here with me? It doesn't make any sense the more I think about it," I ask, trying to ignore any pain I can hear in his words. Ignore that it mirrors my own pain, and forget that I can see his own loneliness reflected in his eyes and words.

"I sent them to you and kept them alive for you," he tells me, and I want to call him out on lying, but I can't. I know he is telling me the truth, I see it in his eyes. I've seen him lie to me enough to pick up on it now. Plus, I don't think the guys could have escaped without help, and Melody would have told me if it were her.

"But why?" I demand, and he looks away.

"Let me tell you something, and I promise if you still want the answer . . . I will tell you," he asks, and I shrug.

"It's not like I can escape you here, so go on," I say, waving a hand at the circle of smoke we are inside. He frowns, but doesn't call me out on it.

"My mother was a happy woman once. She had a good life, and was mated to a fire dragon guard. One day after she found out she was pregnant, my father was killed protecting your mother and father from an attack. My mother kept the pregnancy a secret, knowing I would be in danger if anyone knew who I really was. She left me with my adoptive parents to keep me safe. She was one of the selected, and one of the last ice dragons. It was too dangerous to have me close to her and keep me hidden at the same time. She was happy with her life, seeing me in secret when she could. She was happy with her close childhood friends bringing me up, and it likely would have stayed like that forever . . . but then your mother was killed," he *pauses and shakes his head as snow starts falling from his hands.*

"We all know what happened after that," I say.

"Yes, your father's side of the story," he says bitterly, and I just nod, almost wanting to hear the side he has been told. I want to know what makes him so sure about following his mother's orders while they sit on the throne I'm meant to be on. I have a feeling Thorne isn't in control at all, just being used by his mother for what she wants.

"My mother was commanded to marry an old man, a king twice her age. She was forced to sleep with him, and she had no choice in any of it. I bet your father never told you that, huh?" he growls.

"She got to be queen, and from what I remember, she liked her power, but I didn't know she was forced. For that I'm sorry, but you are punishing me for something I had no control over," I say, struggling to feel sorry for the person who started the fire rebellion and ordered her son to kill my father. Who most likely ordered her sister to kill my intended mate.

"Don't be sorry, you have no idea! No idea what is going on or what works are in play," he turns away from me, running his hands through his hair.

"No, but I know you're a murderer! I know you killed

my father!" I spit out, losing all sympathy for him when I picture my father dead on his throne.

"I didn't," he says quietly, but it shocks me to my core, just the same as if he'd shouted the words. I stumble back, all the hate I feel for him, all the times I've pictured killing him for what he has done flashing across my mind. He still betrayed me, but he didn't kill my father . . . how did that not happen?

"What?" I ask.

"I was meant to kill him, but when I looked into his eyes, I saw you. I saw the girl I sat telling stories to about my bad past, and how she made me laugh in the darkness. The brave girl who lost so much but didn't let it corrupt her. I saw the innocence and the beauty of his daughter. The daughter I couldn't get out of my head, and I couldn't do it," he admits, and I step back in shock.

"Who did?" I ask, seeing the truth in his eyes as he looks up at me.

"My mother, and I didn't stop her. You should hate me for that," he tells me. So, Tatarina is the one that should be on the throne, she is the one that killed the last king. It makes no sense for her to put Thorne on the throne, unless it was because of his blood. Yet, that wouldn't make anyone respect him.

"Why do you want me to hate you?" I ask him, and

he doesn't answer me. He only stares, a hopeless stare which says more than I want to know.

"Why do you listen to her? You know she is evil, right? You can choose to be good, to be different, Thorne," I beg him. His eyes glaze over, the silver almost glowing, and it reminds me so much of Jace that it hurts. But Thorne is different, darker, and more messed-up than anyone I know. It makes me want to fix him, help him, because I have a feeling he isn't all bad. I can feel it inside of me, and it's not something I can ignore anymore. I feel a connection to him, like I do Elias, Korbin, and Dagan. Yet, I have no idea what it means, and it makes no sense. Being connected to any of them means death.

"You're asking me to choose you over my family," he whispers.

"I'm asking you to choose the side for good, to choose someone that could care," I say, my voice catching.

"Could care? Issy don't lie to a liar. You care more than you can even admit to yourself," he chuckles darkly, and everything becomes hazy.

"How are you connected to me?" I ask, feeling myself falling backwards into the smoke, and I can't see him anymore. I just feel him near me.

"Fate," is the last word I hear him whisper before darkness takes over.

. . .

I BLINK MY EYES OPEN, hearing my phone ringing, and am momentarily blinded by the light blasting through a gap in my curtains; it's in my eyes. I pick the phone up, seeing Hallie's name flashing on the bright screen and answer it.

"How was the date?" she asks straight away, sounding like an excited bunny. *How is she so happy this damn early?*

"Erm . . .," I say, blushing when I think back to the date, and everything comes flashing back. I can't believe what happened last night, but I wouldn't change it.

"You totally slept with hottie number two, didn't you?" Hallie asks, laughing.

"Why is Korbin number two?" I ask, curious and not answering her. She knows, I don't need to confirm it.

"Height. Elias is the tallest, then Korbin, and Dagan is the shortest, which isn't saying much, as they are all built like towers you just want to climb," she says, making me laugh.

"You have that right," I say, groaning as I fall back on my bed and look up at the ceiling. Things were a little awkward between Korbin and me when he drove us home last night and walked me to my room. He kissed me, making me want to invite him into my room, but Jules came out and checked on us.

"Any plans for today?" Hallie asks, and I hear the sound of beeping in the background.

"Nope, I don't know what the guys do on Sundays, but I want to eat junk food. Oh, and catch up on *I'm a Celebrity, Get Me Out Of Here* and then read, and read, and read," I say, knowing I need to clear my head of everything I learnt from the dream last night. I need to clear my head in general, and remember who I am, who the guys I'm falling for are. This isn't a fairy tale where the curse is broken in the end and we all have a happy ending . . . No, this is a nightmare, and they will pay the price. Everything is so seriously messed up. I was meant to make the guys remember, not fall for any of them. Yet, I've slept with Korbin, and I damn well know how I feel for him; it sure isn't nothing. I can't keep my thoughts off the others, and the man I thought I hated, now I'm just confused about. *These kinds of thoughts are why I need a reading day to escape.*

"Oh my god, it's the finale tomorrow. You totally need to catch up, so we can discuss who will win! Have a good day, hun," she says, and I hear someone shouting for her in the background.

"Later," I say and put the phone down. I pick up my dressing gown, put it on, and go to the bathroom. I brush my teeth, and run my fingers through my hair, just leaving it down and sliding my slippers on as I leave my room.

"Hey," I say when I run half away down the stairs and see Elias walking up. I pause when he gets closer, leaning sideways on the bannister.

"What did you do to your hands?" I ask, seeing the blood.

"Nothing," he mutters the word quietly, but the tone makes it clear he isn't telling me. He must have been working out, as he is dripping with sweat, his hair pushed roughly out of his eyes. He only has shorts on, so I can see all the tattoos that cover his chest. I want to reach out and touch him, to trace the red dragon design. I want to ask him what the symbols on his heart mean.

"Do you like tattoos?" he asks me, following my eyes to where I'm looking. I don't breathe as he leans into me, pressing me against the side of the stairs. I don't hold back, moving my hands onto his chest over his heart, and tracing the symbols like my body wants me to.

"What are these?" I ask him, looking up when he

stays silent. He is just staring at me, his blue eyes blazing with something.

"Kiss me, and I'll tell you," he promises, a devilish smirk on his lips.

"Eli," I breathe out. I can't believe myself when I inch closer, moving my face just below his. Every part of me wants to kiss him, but I feel like that's cheating on Korbin. That I'm betraying him, somehow, even though we never spoke about being serious. Even though he is likely going to hate me when he remembers who I am.

"Your choice," he whispers, his warm breath blowing across my lips. I close my eyes once more, just breathing in his smoky scent.

"I . . . can't. Korbin and I—" I start to say, but he presses a finger on my lips, stopping me. I open my eyes, seeing he's watching me seriously. He moves his finger, sliding it slowly down my chin and to my neck as he speaks. Every space where our skin connects sends shivers through me. It's like every touch of his skin is branded against my own.

"I don't mind sharing, so you being with Korbin isn't going to prevent me from wanting you," he tells me. He pulls away, walking up the stairs while I try to get some oxygen back into my body. Once Elias is out of view, my dragon perks up, pressing herself into my mind, and making it nearly impossible to move.

"We need to fly, it's been too long," she whines.

"I know, I'm sorry. I've just been distracted," I explain to her. It's not like I don't want to fly, I could use the time to myself.

"Now, I need to fly," she demands this time, even going far enough to push into my mind a little, and ice slides across my palms. I shake my hands, seeing the ice drip onto the floor, and hope no one sees it before it melts.

"Fine." I shut her away, groaning that my day of catching up on TV is gone. Instead, it looks like I'm taking a hike through the woods, and then a flight around the cold mountains.

"Good morning, Isola," Jules says, walking down the stairs. I turn to face her with a smile.

"I'm about to go to the shops, do you want to come? I've never seen boys eat as much as our guests do," she chuckles and walks past me to put her coat on.

"No, thanks, I have a day of books, and drooling over the hot guys in them, planned," I lie, and she laughs, pulling her keys out of her bag.

"Wait, I left a bag in the boot when I went shopping with Dagan, can I just go and get it?" I ask her, holding out my hand for her keys.

"Sure, I could use checking the fridge once more before I leave. You never know, I could have left something off my list," she says, sliding the keys into my hand. I slide my boots on, pulling my dressing gown tighter around myself as I walk out of the house and to the car. I pop the boot open, picking up the daggers and putting them inside a spare plastic bag Jules always leaves inside the car. *Thank god for the ban on free plastic bags in England, that's all I can say.* I walk back into the house to find Jules waiting in the hallway, looking through her bag. I slip my boots off and hand her the keys.

"Okay, hunny, see you later tonight," she says, eyeing my plastic bag for a second, before she walks out the door. I watch through the small glass window until her car pulls away and drives off before getting ready. I pull my dressing gown off, leaving my pajamas on as I will just have to take them off anyway. *No magic clothes here.* I pull my wellies, thick coat, and hat on before stepping outside, still holding the plastic bag. I look up, seeing the dark clouds and smelling the rain in the air. It's actually a good thing; the rain will hide my dragon well when we fly up. I shut the door and start walking towards the woods, keeping an eye out around me to make sure no one is following. Once it's just me and the trees, I look down at my tree mark on my hand. I miss Bee, even though we didn't get that much time together. It just feels like it's been such a long time since I've seen her. It's almost like I can feel our bond growing weaker by the day.

"Do you miss Bee? Can you sense her?" I ask my dragon, wondering what the bond to Bee is like for her.

"Bee is bonded to you like I am, but she is not bonded to me. She is your human side, not your dragon side, Isola," she explains to me.

"I understand, that's why I miss her as much as I do," I say.

"Like you miss me," she replies sadly.

"I will never lose you," I reply, feeling a wave of warmth and love come from her. I smile, walking more quickly through the woods. About an hour later, I get to the clearing I used to shift in with Jace.

"Jace," my dragon whispers.

"I miss him, too, so much more now that I'm here and surrounded with our memories. Do you think he would hate me for moving on?" I ask her, being that she is the only one that remembers him. Even if she is an animal that relies on instincts for everything,

she still loved and bonded with him in the same ways I did. She still felt heartbreak, she felt the same fear of being alone like I did.

"*No, it was never your fate to be with just one,*" she replies, sounding so sure of herself.

"*How do you know anything about fate, dragon?*" I ask her, and she just laughs.

"*Seers and dragons came from the same land. Fate brought us all into existence. It's not what I know, it's what I feel.*" She says, gentle almost. I open the plastic, pulling out one of the daggers. I flip it over, looking closely at the fire dragon on it. I know I won't get any answers from the dagger, but I still commit the crest on the dagger to memory. Someone came after me, and I want to know who. I pick the other dagger up, holding them both at my sides and look over at the tree about fifty feet away from me. I spin around, throwing both the daggers at the same time and they slam into the tree, buried to the hilt.

"*Now shift,*" she tells me. Our conversation makes me wonder what else my dragon knows but decides not to tell me. I pull my coat off, followed by my boots, and finally my pajamas. I walk away from the tree I leave them near, and take a deep breath, smelling for any humans nearby and finding none. I open my arms, calling my dragon, and white mist appears in front of me slowly, swallowing me inside of it. She takes over with a roar that shakes all of the trees near us, and then she stretches her wings out, ice falling off them onto the grass. She looks up at the skies, her sense of freedom improving even my bad mood. She then lifts herself off the ground and shoots into the sky.

CHAPTER
SIXTEEN
ISOLA

My dragon lands in the clearing many hours later with a huff, her annoyance at the dark skies and knowledge that she needs to let me back flooding her thoughts. The rain pours down on us, soaking my dragon, and I know it will be worse when I'm in human form.

"*Again . . . soon?*" she asks me as she lets me shift back, my human form kneeling on the cold ground, naked and freezing everything off as my wet, cold hair drips down my body. I look up at the skies, just as the rain stops slowly.

"*Soon,*" I reply and stand up, freezing when I hear a branch snap somewhere near me. I don't move, looking around as I open my senses. I jump to my right when a shadow of a man steps out from behind the trees where my clothes are hidden. He walks into the clearing, pausing as he holds my clothes in his arms. His eyes widen and quickly look away. *Shit, I'm naked and not the kinda naked I'd like to be with Dagan.*

"Dagan," I say his name carefully, very aware it's unlikely he didn't just see me shift back from a dragon. He watches me, his black hair dripping rain water down his face, his blue eyes almost glowing in the darkness. His white shirt is wet, his jeans too, and they stick to his impressive body as he breathes deeply. It's the only sign he is even alive, the movement of his chest. I hope he didn't see me shift, but when he meets my eyes, the fear is too hard to just avoid. *He knows, and how the hell do I explain that?*

"What . . . the . . . hell?" he asks slowly, his usual calm voice is replaced with a nervous, gruff one. He keeps his eyes locked on my face, and not looking anywhere else. He doesn't look scared, or even that shocked . . . but fearful. *Which is understandable, I mean most people would just go running in the other direction, screaming.*

"Can I have my clothes and then explain?" I ask, and he nods, walking closer and handing me my clothes slowly before stepping away again. It's awkward as I quickly get dressed, sliding my boots and coat on over my pajamas. I squeeze my wet hair, the rain dripping on the ground before shaking it and pushing it out of my face. He just waits the whole time silently. It's unnerving to me.

"You're a dragon?" he asks finally.

"Yes . . ." I say, and he steps back, shaking his head.

"A . . . dragon . . . dragon," he mutters, rubbing his lip ring between his lips and not really making much sense, "dragons aren't real. Just damn fairy tales, but that doesn't explain what I just saw."

"Do you want to sit down or something?" I ask, making him laugh. A sarcastic and mean laugh as he glares at me.

"No, I don't want to sit down, Isola! I want you to explain what you are! How dragons even exist?" he says, frustrated. "How one minute this huge dragon flies out the sky, and the next, white shit appears, and you are there. Naked."

"Technically, what *we* are," I say, just needing to point that out, but regret it when his eyes widen in shock. I try to think back to the paranormal books where the main guy usually has to explain to the female main character how she is one of them. *How did they do it?*

"I'm not a dragon, I would have noticed that," he huffs, waving a hand at his body.

"Erm, well, you are, but a seer has blocked your dragon away in your mind. Made you forget who you are and your past," I say, and for a second I think he might believe me, but then he steps back.

"You're crazy," he tries to walk away, and I hold my hand out, making a wall of ice appear in front of him, and he stops walking just before he would have hit it. He turns, looking at my hand and back at the wall of ice.

"What the fuck?" he exclaims, stepping away from it, shaking his head.

"You need to believe me, I'm tired of trying to do things to make you remember who you are, Dagan," I say.

"Like what?"

"When I asked you about your parents? Your childhood, it was like a robot repeating a story with no details," I say, and he shakes his head.

"You're mad," he says.

"Nope, I'm not. So, Dagan, what was your favourite ice cream as a child? Where did you hide when you played hide and seek? Where did your parents take you when you did something good in school?" I ask, and he gives me a confused look.

"I . . . I."

"You don't know, because it's not real. The real Dagan was brought up in a whorehouse, the bastard child of a fire guard, and his mother was killed. I know this because your brother told me, because I met you as a child," I say, and he glares, a glare that almost makes me want to run away from him. But I don't, I hold my ground. I need him to see I'm telling him the truth. I need him to remember.

"I need to tell Elias and Korbin about this, about you," he says and starts pacing. I stay silent for a while, letting him pace as my wall of ice melts slowly, and the moon starts to come out. It's getting dark quickly, and we should get back home, but Dagan is still pacing.

"They won't believe it, and they are dragons, too. Can you stop pacing and freaking out for a second?" I ask, placing my hands on my hips.

"What do you suggest I do? Just act like you don't turn into a massive blue ice dragon, and you're not telling me I'm one?" he asks me sarcastically.

"That would be great, yes," I say, nodding, and he gives me a nasty look.

"Look, it's getting dark, and I'm worn out from flying all day. Let's go back home, and you can freak all you want there. Go ahead, and tell anyone you want, no one will believe you," I say walking past him, and pausing before I get to the trees.

"When you want the real truth of who you are, you know where I am," I tell him, thinking I've heard that in a book somewhere, and it's good advice. I walk off into the woods after one more look, seeing the angry look crossing over his face as he stares. After walking for a while, trying to avoid logs and rocks, I hear Dagan stalking behind me. I turn to see him looking at the ground. Clearly, he is thinking but likely doesn't want to talk to me yet. *I guess it's a big shock.* I turn back, walking to the light from the house in the distance, and when we get there, Dagan walks past me through the front door and straight up the stairs. I shut the door, sighing against it for a moment until Korbin walks out of the kitchen with a bowl of popcorn.

"Long day?" he asks, eyeing my dirt-covered clothes and messy hair, and then to Dagan walking up the stairs.

"I went for a hike, Dagan came too," I explain, and his eyes narrow.

"Right, I see how it is," he says, accusing me of something I haven't even done.

"Kor–" I get out, but he cuts me off, pissing me off.

"Don't," he says, walking up the stairs, and I just close my eyes, wondering if this day could get any worse. The house phone starts ringing, and I run over, picking it up.

"Hello?" I ask in a tired voice, I just want to go to sleep and pray this day couldn't get worse.

"Hello, is this the home of Jules Donald?" a man asks, the sound of beeping and people talking filling the background.

"Yes, I don't know if she is in as I've just gotten home, but I can take a message," I say, picking the pen up off the side and going to grab the paper when the man speaks.

"Madam, Miss Donald is in hospital, and I would like you, or her next of kin, to come in. She asked for an Isola Dragice," he says, making my heart pound against my chest. This can't be happening, not Jules.

"That's me, I'll be right there, is she okay?" I ask.

"I can't tell you any more on the phone. Please don't worry and come in," he says, and I say goodbye before putting the phone down. I run up the stairs, knocking on Elias's door and waiting. He opens it up a few moments later, looking like I just woke him up, with his messy hair, and just his pajama shorts on.

"What's up?" he asks.

"Jules is in hospital, and I need a ride there. Dagan and Korbin aren't talking to me, so could you please take me?" I ask, and he nods, reaching for a hoodie off the back of the door and pulling it over his head, hiding the body I can't even focus on because I'm so worried about Jules.

"Yeah, anything for you, princess. Is she okay? What happened?" he asks, and walks past me out the door.

"I don't know," I admit, and he slides his hand into mine, squeezing once before letting go. I wait for him to get his coat and some keys off the side.

"I'm sure Korbin won't mind us borrowing his car," Elias smirks, holding the keys up in the air.

"I'm pretty sure he will," I say, remembering how angry he looked, how he judged the situation wrong and walked away. I walk up to the car, waiting for Elias to unlock it and then getting in. Elias gets in, doing his seatbelt at the same time as me before starting the car.

"So, what happened to Jules to get her in the hospital?" he asks.

"I don't know, they didn't tell me much, just that she asked for me. I'm all they had to call. She basically brought me up, so she is all the family I have in a way," I explain, and he nods, not taking his eyes off the road. Thankfully it's only twenty minutes' drive to the hospital, and there's no traffic around.

"Okay, another question. What happened with Korbin and Dagan?" Elias asks, and I look out the window.

"I don't want to talk about it," I mutter.

"Come on, princess, you can trust me," he says cheekily, and I shake my head, hating how he can make me smile.

"Fine. Korbin thinks something happened between Dagan and me today, when it didn't," I say, still cross about how angry he got without talking to me. I hate being judged for something I haven't done. I can't say I hadn't thought about doing it, but yeah . . . I *hadn't*.

"Okay, have you ever heard the term reverse harem?" he asks me, surprising me a little.

"I read a lot, and my favourite is a series about demons," I say. "But you can't be suggesting . . . and how do you even know about reverse harems?" I blurt out, feeling my cheeks getting red.

"I read, and it's something I'm interested in, with the right people," he says, shocking me silent.

"It wouldn't work, you guys are all too posses-sive," I say, knowing dragons are naturally posses-sive about those they consider theirs. They see their mates like treasures, and they don't like to share those. Like my dragon seems to think they are all hers, and I know she would lose her shit on me if I tried to date anyone else. I never got why she put a claim to them in the first place, why she calls them mine. I want to ask her, but I can't with Elias watching me so closely.

"Yeah, I am. I don't know why, but the idea of anyone touching you . . . It's not good, princess," he admits, tightening his hands on the steering wheel. "Then I think about you and Korbin and Dagan . . . I wouldn't hurt them for loving you."

"You wouldn't?" I ask, curious.

"No. But I know you're not ready to be with us all, and to be honest, none of us are even close to figuring out what is between us," he tells me, and honestly, as I meet his blue eyes, I know he is right.

"What did the doctor say?" Elias asks, using his shoulder to open the door as he carries two hot teas in his hands. The door shuts behind him as I look at Jules on the bed, plugged into dozens of wires and looking as pale as the bedsheets. I wipe a tear away, numbly repeating what the human doctor told me.

"Jules had a heart attack and fell over, banging her head. They said they have her in a medically induced coma to stop the swelling on her brain before waking her up," I say, struggling with the worry I feel for Jules.

"Here, a cup of tea always helps everything. Or that's what Jules told me two days ago," he says, making me chuckle.

"Yeah, she is British through and through, thinking a cup of tea fixes everything," I mutter, but he hears me.

"I never really liked it," he says, sipping his drink and pulling a face.

"Shhh, don't let her hear you say that," I say, smiling. Elias always knows how to make me smile somehow. I drink my tea, still holding onto her hand with mine. I knew I'd see her die one day, as a human her lifespan is so much shorter than mine. It still hurts, it still crushes me to know she will be gone, and every connection to a massive part of my life is just gone with her. I stand up, putting the cup down and walking out of the room, not really thinking or looking where I'm going.

"Isola, wait!" I hear Elias shout, but I can't listen as I start running and going down corridor after corridor until I find some stairs. I open the door, running up the stairs and getting to the very top, and to the emergency-only door. I pull it open, running out onto the roof and just stopping. The view is amazing up here: hills, trees, and lit-up houses for miles to see. The stars above make a beautiful backdrop, but all I can think about is how much pain happened in this world because I don't belong here. I can feel it, I always felt it. This isn't my world, and I feel trapped here. Haunted by ghosts.

"Isola . . ." I hear Elias say behind me, the sound of the door shutting behind me makes me jump. I turn, seeing him standing a few steps away from me. There's such tension between us, so many unanswered questions running across his eyes, such passion. I want to run to him, let him hold me like I know he would. But I don't, instead I take a step back, protecting myself from doing anything I know I might regret. Not that I would regret being in his arms, but I would regret the curse taking any price for any of my actions. I have already risked Korbin, and I know him hating me now is only a slight fraction of what he will feel when he remembers.

"Tell me, what is it you're hiding? What are you running from?" he asks me, his deep and seductive voice making me close my eyes.

"You will be the one running if I tell you what I am," I say, meaning every word.

"I don't run, I will never run from you," he says, a promise laced into his words. I pull my coat off, chucking it on the floor and kicking my boots off as he gives me a confused look. I laugh, a long laugh as I call my dragon, and shift. He stumbles back when I land on the roof as my dragon stretches out her wings. She turns her head to the side, seeing the ice dripping off each little spike on her wings, before turning back to Elias. I watch him, fully expecting him to run from me, but he doesn't. He stands up and walks slowly to my dragon, each step full of a confidence I would expect the old Elias to have. When he gets closer, he holds a hand out, and my dragon pushes her nose into his hand, a purr vibrating through her.

"*Mine,*" she whispers, and I don't disagree with her, because it feels wrong to say she isn't right. My dragon steps back, feeling my need to shift, and I close my eyes, pulling my human form back. I look up, my long hair falling around me as Elias stands utterly still. I pick my coat up, seeing my torn clothes on the floor but once my coat is done up, it's good enough. *Only a little bit cold.*

"You're a dragon? A shifter, or whatever you call yourself?" he asks, and I nod, not wanting to tell him he is one, too, as that didn't work so well with Dagan.

"What else can you do?" he asks, reaching into his pocket and pulling out his cigarettes. He puts one in his mouth, lighting it with a lighter, and then resting against the door.

"Ice and snow," I say, holding my hands into the

air and closing my eyes. I focus on the clouds above, freezing them slowly and then open my eyes.

"I don't see anything . . ." he drawls.

"Just wait," I chuckle, just as it starts to snow. Slowly at first, and the wind starts blowing it around us.

"Amazing," he says, his voice full of wonder, and he keeps smoking. We are both silent, both of us close to freezing until he finishes his cigarette and puts it out under his boot. He walks over, stopping right in front of me.

"Any more secrets you want to tell me?" he asks, and he watches me so closely for my reaction that it hurts when the lie slips from my mouth.

"Maybe, but not yet," I answer, and he nods.

"You don't trust me," he says, and for the first time, hurt appears in his eyes. I can see it and he steps back, walking to the door.

"Eli, it's—"

"You don't trust me, and I'm not going to make you, *princess*," he says and opens the door, slamming it closed behind him. I look up at the star-filled skies, the dark clouds, and the snow falling slowly. I mess everything up, and I don't know how to stop doing it.

"So, why are the sexy guys annoyed with you?" Hallie asks me as I open my packet of crisps and lean back in my seat, following her gaze to Dagan, Korbin, and Elias who are sitting at another table. Each one of them has ignored me since the weekend, but all for different reasons. Korbin thinks I'm sleeping with Dagan, and clearly can't deal with me. Dagan knows I'm a dragon and overall looks freaked out by me. And Elias . . . well, I think is just working out what I'm still hiding from him, but at least he isn't freaked out like Dagan is. I'm actually not sure about Elias at the moment, what he is thinking anyway, but I don't tell Hallie any of this.

"I don't know, they are just moody," I say, and then stuff my face with food and hope it makes me feel better. It doesn't, but hey, the chocolate buttons are just amazing.

"How is Jules?" Hallie asks.

"She woke up two days ago and is a little groggy, she will need a lot of medical care, but they think she will make a full recovery," I tell her.

"I'm glad, I know how much you care for her," she tells me, and I nod, not really wanting to speak about Jules. I know I have to return to Dragca, so I can't look after her long-term like I wish I could. Like she deserves. Instead, I had to use the stupid amount of human money in my account to buy her a place in a nursing home for when she gets out of the hospital. I hate that it's all I can do.

"Hey, sexy Issy," Michael says, sliding into the seat next to me, and in some ways, I'm thankful for the distraction from my own thoughts and stuff I can't change. Hallie just rolls her eyes, stabbing her fork into her pie. I mentally groan as I turn to face him. He slides his giant arm around my shoulder, pulling me into a side hug. I try to pull away, but he doesn't let for me for a while, making me super uncomfortable.

"Michael, you're hurting me," I say, when he

doesn't let go, squeezing me too tightly, and he does straight away, grinning as he pushes his blonde hair out of the way of his eyes.

"Sorry, I forget how small you are," he comments, using that as an excuse to look down my top and not raise his eyes for far too long. *Urgh.*

"Michael, don't you have an interview with my father tonight? Shouldn't you be . . . I don't know, training or researching, or something other than hitting on Issy?" Hallie asks, cutting in, and I flash her a thankful smile.

"You're working for Hallie's dad?" I ask Michael, moving across my seat and towards Hallie.

"Our parents are good friends, so he offered me a job. It's a brilliant one," he says, and Hallie laughs, but she doesn't say anything as Michael glares at her.

"Shut it," he snaps at her, and she still laughs. It gets seriously awkward as I sit between them, having no idea what they are talking about. I wish I knew what her father does, what she is so sure she doesn't want to do.

"So, erm, how was your weekend?" I ask Michael when there's a very uncomfortable silence between us all for way too long.

"Didn't do much, I'm just looking forward to my

party. You are still coming, right?" he asks, like an excited child.

"Yep," I say, not really wanting to go, but the puppy dog eyes he is doing right now makes me feel a little guilty. I look away, seeing Dagan, Korbin, and Elias all watching me, wearing matching faces of anger. I want to get up and go to sit with them, explain myself to each of them, but I can't. I've already messed up with Dagan, and risked the curse with Korbin. Even with Elias if I'm honest with myself. I might not have kissed him since Dragca, and he might be hurt because of me right now, but there's something between us. *Some princess I am, making the guards lose their dragons because I can't control my hormones.* The bell rings, snapping me out of it, and I quickly stand up.

"Time for class," I say, walking away, but Michael grabs my arm as he stands, roughly pulling me to him.

"Let go," I say carefully, not liking how strong he is, and how my dragon hisses in my mind. I look up as he grins.

"I only wanted a hug, sexy Issy," he says playfully, and I pull my arm away.

"You should wait for me to offer, not demand.

Goodbye, Michael," I tell him, seeing his bright-red face as he glares at me. Hallie links her arm with mine, walking out of the dinner hall at my side. I rub my arm, looking behind me to see Michael still watching me, anger flittering in his eyes. Humans and dragons never date, because the human always gets obsessed. It was one of the things Jace made sure I knew, not only for my protection but for my understanding of why guys like Michael won't leave me alone.

"You should stay away from Michael, he is pretty obsessed with you. I don't want to see what he would do when he realises you're not interested," Hallie tells me, looking back at him when I turn around.

"I plan to stay away, don't worry," I reply.

"So, you're not going to the party?" she asks, relief flittering over her face.

"I will if the guys go, they wouldn't let anything happen to me, and I need to get them to speak to me," I say.

"Why? They might be sexy, but so are you. You don't need to chase them," she says gently.

"I'm not chasing them, it's complicated," I say, and she smiles.

"Good, I'm not having you chase anyone," she says, and I quickly pull her in for a hug. She hugs me back, laughing.

"What's that for?" she asks.

"For being a good friend. Whatever happens, I'm your friend," I tell her, and she gives me a slightly confused look as I pull away.

"What would happen?" she asks, and part of me wishes I could explain all this to her. Explain that I'm a dragon, and I have to go back to Dragca soon. That I won't see her for a long time, and I might die trying to save the world I was born in. Not that I can tell her anything, only enjoy the little time I have with a true friend now.

"Nothing, I'm being silly," I reply, lying.

"Come on, you weirdo, it's Mr. Dread's class, and you know how much of an arsehole he is if we are late," she says, tugging me along to class.

"Isola!" I hear my name shouted as I walk out of the school, and I look through the students, seeing Dagan walking through them and towards me like a man on a mission. He looks stressed, his black hair looks like it has had his hands run through it a million times. I look down, seeing the shadows under his eyes and the tight-lipped expression he is giving me. He has a black coat on, tight black jeans, and a grey jumper underneath. It makes him look like a normal guy, a hot god-type guy, but still not someone I'd expect to be a dragon.

"Hey," I say, wondering what he wants when he nods his head to the left of me and walks around me, not stopping once. I follow him, looking over when I hear Elias's bike roaring, and seeing him driving out of the car park. I don't see Korbin's car, so I think he must have left without Dagan. Dagan walks to the bus stop, sitting down on the empty seat as students walk past us. There are three other students around when I sit down next to him, but they have their headphones in, or they aren't paying attention to us. Both of us are silent for a long time, just watching nothing. I just wait for something from him, any sign that I haven't messed everything up when I need his help.

"I have fucked-up dreams," he says quietly.

"Yeah?" I mumble.

"Yeah, kitty cat, dreams that make me believe what you are telling me," he says and reaches over, taking my hand in his and linking our fingers. His hand feels warm, rough and right.

"Do you believe me?" I ask him.

"Yes, I believe you. Or I want to," he admits, sending relief crashing through me.

"I need you all to remember, only you can help me. Or I'm not going to make it long, and people will suffer in our home world if I don't try to fix things,"

"Tell me some things you know about me? About my home land?" he asks.

"Honestly? We only knew each other for a month or so. You are a dragon guard, and I'm a royal. Even though I haven't known you that long, I know a lot. I know you're one of the bravest, most stubborn men I've ever met. You are cocky, protective, and sometimes even charming," I chuckle when he grins.

"Seems you liked me."

"Sometimes," I laugh, but it dies away when the seriousness of everything rushes back. "Dragca needs me, needs us. I'm meant to be on the throne, meant to be ruling and uniting everyone. But right now, it's got Thorne, one of my old guards on it."

"Old guard?" he asks.

"Longer story, you kinda dislike him. Elias hates him, but I see something in him, even though most of me hates him for the things he has done," I say quietly, and Dagan leans over, moving a little bit of my hair over my shoulder, before trailing his fingers down my side.

"You are so much of the light, you know that?" he asks me, staring at me strangely.

"What?" I ask, wondering why he would say such a strange thing.

"In my dreams, a girl I've never seen before, tells me you are the light. All the light left to save us from dying in the dark," he tells me, and I stare wide-eyed at him.

"What does the girl look like?" I ask quickly.

"Honestly, green. Like a green Barbie doll, and the size of one, too," he says, making my heart pound. Bee told him something, I don't know how it's possible, but she did.

"A lot of things are so uncertain for us, maybe it would be best if you got up and walked away. Lived a life as a human, and I go back to my world, face what I'm running from alone," I say, and he shakes his head.

"Every little bit of me tells me I could never let you do that alone, Isola," he bites out, anger clouding his blue eyes.

"Dagan, get Korbin and Elias, and go. I can't do

this, I can't let you try and fight with me," I suddenly realise. I can't lose them, and taking them back to Dragca would mean I could. They are safe here, safer than another place, even if they don't remember who they are.

"All I know is that I want to be close to you, and this distance between us is driving me fucking insane. I'm with you, no matter what," he says as the bus turns up, but neither of us moves as we stare at each other. Our faces are inches apart as he leans closer, and a car beeping makes us shoot apart before he can kiss me. We shouldn't anyway, no matter how disappointed I feel.

"You shouldn't want me, we can't be together. There's a curse, a curse that says you will lose your dragon if you fall in love with me," I blurt out loudly to him and then look around quickly, noticing all the people have, thankfully, gotten on the bus, so they didn't hear us.

"Apparently, I've already lost my dragon, so what more could any curse do to me for doing this," he says and moves over, slamming his lips onto mine. I slide my hand into his hair, fully accepting his kiss, loving how his lip ring feels as it slides across my own lips. He groans, pulling me as close as we can get without me climbing in his lap, sliding his hands into my hair.

"Kitty cat, I feel like I've wanted to do that forever," he whispers against my lips and then kisses me again before I can answer. Maybe he has wanted to kiss me for a long time because I know in this moment, I've wanted to kiss him for just as long.

"It's about time, I've been waiting in this place for an hour. Go to sleep on time please," Melody's voice comes through the haze, and I open my eyes to see her standing over me as I lie on the floor.

"I made the mistake of checking on my future girl-friend and her life, only to see her with another guy," she says, as I stare up at her.

"Is she not out of the closet yet then?" I ask.

"Nope, but I've seen us together. It was my first vision, and the only one I've had about myself," she tells me. I always wondered if she sees a lot of her own future, and how creepy that must be.

"You must be excited to meet her then," I say.

"We already met, but it's complicated as she doesn't

160

remember me. Anyways, you should get up as we don't have much time as you didn't go to sleep," she says, offering me a hand. I stand up, looking around at the trees and more trees that surround us. I look up, seeing two moons, so I know it's Dragca.

"What is this a warning of?" I ask her, ignoring her whining about me not going to sleep on time. I didn't know she was waiting for me, it's been over a week since she last came to my dreams.

"Wait for it," she waves a hand behind me, and I turn, seeing myself running through the woods in the distance, three men are chasing after me. I look desperate, broken, covered in blood in a long dress that catches on everything I run past. I watch myself run, and I step forward, wanting to save myself. A person walks in after the guards and me, following them but not looking in any rush, dark smoke trailing after her cloak on the ground. The smoke slides up the trees next to her, burning them into dust. I've never seen anything like it, and it honestly terrifies me.

"What happened to me?" I ask quietly.

"I don't know, I only see this one after you come for me. There will be no more warnings for a while, sister," she says sadly, and then I hear myself scream. The scream goes on and on, and then there's a loud bang that makes Melody and me cover our ears. Fire shoots up in the air,

blasting out in every direction and heading straight for us. It burns all the trees in its path, and blue lights come out the trees, floating up into the air. I can feel their sorrow; the lights seem to look into my soul. The fire goes around us, like we're immune to it and yet part of me wants to stop it.

"This moment feels massive, yet, I don't understand it," Melody admits, and I look over at her, seeing fear in her eyes for the first time. She has always come across so fearless, so sure of herself, but not right now. And that scares me, more than anything has scared me for a long time.

"Melody . . . Dagan and Elias know what I am but don't remember. My relationship with all of them is advancing more than it should. Thorne is . . . well, I don't know, but he confuses me. He didn't kill our father," I ramble out.

"I know, I see it," she taps her head.

"Tell me what to do, how to make them remember," I ask.

"I can't. What has to happen, will happen, and they will remember because of it," she says, a tear dropping from her right eye.

"Because of what?" I ask.

"Because of the emotion. The hate, fear, and the love.

It's the only way, and I'm so sorry I can't stop it," she says, stepping closer, and placing her hand on mine.

"I need you, and Thorne does. Don't forget about us," she asks.

"I wouldn't forget, not unless you make me," I joke, making her smile for a second, but it soon fades.

"The curse will fall, and so will you, but remember, Isola. Remember what you have to fight for," she says, pulling me into a hug, and holding on tight. I return the hug, feeling strange about hugging my sister I've never known.

"I'm going to show you something you must tell Thorne when you have a moment alone with him. A real moment, not a dream, and you will know when," she begs me so seriously.

"How can you show me?" I ask her.

"By using all my power, it just hurts me a little bit, and I will sleep for a few days. No biggie," she says, shrugging a shoulder, and moving to stand right in front of me.

"No biggie? That sounds big, I don't want you hurt. You're my sister," I say, grabbing her hands.

"And that's exactly why I must show you this, you must make Thorne see the truth because I can only show you, and he won't believe me. My mother showed me *this, just before Tatarina killed her, and I know it's the only way to save everyone," she says.*

"How can one vision save everyone? And I'm sorry about your mother," I ask.

"Because it shows you who the real villain is, who really killed both of our mothers," she says and puts her hands on my head. A blinding light bursts into my mind. When I can see again, it's like I'm floating above the ground in an empty hut. The hut has stone floors, a fire in the fireplace, and a small table. The door opens and Tatarina walks in, a much younger version of her anyway. She is stunning, a perfect image of an ice dragon with her long white-blonde hair and pale-blue eyes. I'm sure her eyes aren't that pale anymore, I've never seen them like this anyway. Two other people come into the room, a couple about her age, and the man with brown hair shuts the door.

"We have to kill the queen. She is evil; I've told you this, but I can't do it. You can get close enough when you go to the castle tomorrow," she says, shocking me. I didn't expect her to say that. I knew she was evil, but to ask someone to kill my mother?

"We would never get close, but I will try because of everything you have told me about her. She tortures dragons and humans, she kills children, and the king hides it because he loves her. She must die," the man

says, and I shake my head, wanting to scream at him that none of this is true, but no sound comes out my mouth.

"Thank you, my friend," Tatarina says, and the door opens again. A little boy runs in with blonde hair, covered in dirt, and blue eyes. He runs up to Tatarina.

"Mummy!" the boy shouts, and when I look closer, I know it's Thorne.

"Go with your parents, we had a good day together, but you can't stay late," Tatarina says, hugging Thorne, who nods and walks over to the couple who open the door. I keep my eyes on the man's face, and I know this is the man that killed my mother. Thorne's adoptive father killed my mother. He knew and lied to me, he made me feel sorry for him and his parents. Bastard. Thorne and his parents leave, shutting the door behind them. Tatarina grins, looking up at the ceiling near where I am floating as if she can see me. She raises her hands, and a dark spirit flies in from a hole in the ceiling. The dark spirit has dark blue skin that almost looks black, black hair, and smoke drifting off its body. It looks just like Bee, a light spirit, only dark-skinned instead. The dark spirit lands on Tatarina's hand, and she grins at it.

"Our plan is starting. We will have the throne and an heir because of my son, who can rule. I will kill the princess and any other ice dragons that stand in our

way. Then we can enact the second part of our plan," she says, and the dark spirit nods. Just before I float away, I hear, "My son will be king, but I will rule. He just doesn't know it yet."

I SLAM AWAKE, my heart pounding against my chest, and it takes me a moment to realise someone has their hands on my shoulders, rubbing their thumbs in a comforting motion. I look up to see Elias looking down at me with worry, his hair is messy, and his t-shirt is all wrinkled. I take deep breaths, breathing in his smoky scent to calm myself down. I'm safe, I'm not there anymore, and the dark spirit is gone. I repeat the same line in my head over and over until I can breathe normally. That vision, or whatever it was, felt so real. It was overwhelming, terrifying, and it makes so much sense. Tatarina planned this all, she planned for my mother to be killed, to become queen, to put Thorne on the throne and control him. *What else has she got planned?*

"You were screaming. I'm sorry, but I had to wake you up," he explains to me, removing his hands and sitting on the edge of my bed. "Bad dreams, princess?" he asks carefully.

"Something like that," I say breathlessly, looking

at my phone and seeing it's only three in the morning.

"Sorry I woke you up," I tell him, and he shrugs.

"I went outside for a cigarette, and I was walking past," he explains.

"Outside? I thought you smoked them in your room," I chuckle.

"Nah, not since Jules walked in on me once. She hit me with her shoe and told me she wouldn't have me smoking in her house," he smirks. "I like the old lady, but she can half hit with that shoe," he tells me, making me laugh.

"That's better, you laughing is much better than seeing you frightened," he says gently.

"It just takes a minute to realise some dreams aren't real," I mutter, and he tilts his head to the side a little. We don't say anything, but I push my hair out of my eyes when it falls and look down at my pajamas. Thank god I'm wearing plain blue ones, and not the ones with cupcakes all over that I almost put on.

"Yeah, I get that, princess," he squeezes my hand and stands up, dropping the notebook he was holding.

"What's that?" I ask, remembering his notebook at Dragca Academy. I wonder if he draws the same type things. It would make sense for him to have the same hobbies, enjoy the same things he always had. He is the same dragon I met, just with a few little changes.

"Here," he offers me the notebook. To my surprise, he walks around the bed, pulling off his leather jacket and boots. He slides into bed next to me, tucking himself in like he sleeps in my bed all the time or something. He rolls on his side, raising an eyebrow at me as he rests his head on his arm.

"Comfy?" I ask sarcastically, and he smirks.

"*Very*," he replies, somehow making one word seem seductive and panty-dropping. *Damn him.* I shake my head, looking back at the notebook to get my eyes off him. I open the first page to see a drawing of me, not what I was expecting at all. It's a beautifully drawn image of me sitting on the school bus, and looking over my shoulder. It's the first time he saw me here on Earth. He makes my eyes look bigger than they are, like I'm a doll or something. My hair is layered down my back in perfect curls, and my face looks perfect, not one imperfection. Which I know isn't true, I know I have a slight dent on the right side of my nose where I broke it falling out of a tree in Dragca when I was seven. I know I have freckles littered across my nose, too, and they spread to my cheeks when it's summer. I'm not perfect, not in any way.

"You make me look pretty, way too pretty," I say, and he chuckles low.

"I don't make you anything other than what you are," he argues. I look back, flipping through the notebook, seeing more and more sketches of myself. All little moments in class, all times when I never saw him even looking at me. I turn over a page and stop, seeing a different drawing. It's a tattoo design, with four red dragons flying around an ice dragon in the center of them. They almost look like they're protecting her. The main dragon looks like mine, and the little ones are all slightly different. There are swirls coming off the ice dragon, connecting them all together, and it's remarkable. I can't look away, I just end up staring at it. I feel Elias slowly look over, to see what I'm so fascinated by.

"I love this," I say, tracing my finger over the design.

"It's yours, I designed it for you. I don't remember when I exactly started drawing it, but it was way before I met you in another notebook and then re-drew it here. Yet somehow I know it's yours," he says, making my heart pound.

"Thank you, Eli," I whisper, tracing the design with my finger.

"I love when you call me that," he says gruffly, his voice almost a whisper like mine. Neither of us say a word, and without communicating, I know neither of us wants to ruin the moment. I can see it when I look over at him, I know him well enough to read it in his eyes. I put the notebook on my side, and then lie down in bed, facing him. I reach up, placing my hand on his cheek, and he closes his eyes at my touch.

"What if I told you that kissing you could trigger a curse? That it could destroy everything you don't even know you have?" I ask him, my words coming out more breathless than I intend them to be.

"A curse?" he asks, frowning at me. As he opens those blue eyes, I find myself instantly lost in them.

"Yes, a curse that was meant to do good for my family, but right now it feels like it's destroying the very family it was meant to protect," I say, meaning every word. *Why does it have to be like this? It's not fair.*

"You're not making much sense, princess," he says, and I shake my head, lowering my head to his chest after he rolls onto his back. I reach over, switching the lamp off, and then placing my hand on his chest.

"Stay the night?" I ask him, not really giving him a choice as I'm already comfy, and don't want to move.

"You don't have to ask, princess," he whispers, kissing my forehead. Only seconds later, darkness makes me fall asleep as I lay listening to his beating heart.

"Someone is knocking on your door. It's too fucking early for me to be a gentleman and answer it for you," a voice grumbles. The feeling of a face pushing into my neck has me blinking my eyes open. I pull myself awake to find Elias practically lying on top of me, and he looks up, his messy hair makes him look cute in an early morning way.

"How much would you hate me if I said how cute you are in the morning?" I ask, and he glares at me, rolling over and pulling a pillow over his head. *Someone doesn't like mornings.*

"Get the door," he groans, his voice muffled by his pillow. I laugh, getting out of bed and walking to the door, opening it a little to see Korbin standing outside.

"Hey?" I ask, sounding like a dork.

"Running? I know we haven't been speaking recently, but I–" he says, and then Eli's loud shout interrupts him.

"Keep it down!"

I look back at Korbin as his whole face tightens, and then he turns, walking away. "Korbin, wait!" I shout, running out the door and down the stairs after him. I catch him just before he gets to the front door, grabbing his arm.

"Let me explain," I plead.

"Explain what? Am I nothing to you? Or was it only me that felt something, Isola?" he fires all the questions quickly at me, never giving me a second to reply.

"Kor, it wasn't nothing. It meant *everything* to me. You have no fucking idea how hard this is for me. What I'm doing, it is killing me as I don't want to hurt anyone," I tell him, and he turns, pushing me lightly into the wall and stepping close. He presses me against the wall as he slides his hand to the back of my neck, and he makes me look up at him. His green eyes blaze as he stares at me. It's almost unnerving to see the emotion in his eyes, but I don't look away. I know he needs to see the same passion in mine, he needs to know that I don't feel nothing. I feel everything, and it frightens me.

"I don't know how to cope with how you look at Dagan and Elias," he admits, his thumb stroking the back of my neck.

"I don't know what I'm doing, only that I can't stay away from any of you," I reply truthfully.

"Then for now, this is how it is, because, fuck, Isola, I can't lose you," he says and slams his mouth onto mine. I moan against his lips, returning the kiss the best I can when he is taking total control, leaving me no break between each punishing kiss. He brushes his lips down my jaw, angling my head with his hand on my neck, and then breaking away.

"Now, get your cute butt back to your room, and get your running gear on," he says, an actual smile on his lips for the first time I've seen this week. He lets me free from against the wall, and I jump when he slaps my ass playfully as I pass him.

"Cheeky," I say, but I can't keep the grin off my face.

"Oh, and Isola?" he stops me when I get to the bottom step.

"Yeah?" I turn to ask.

"Make a lot of noise as you get changed, I don't

think Eli was awake enough yet," he says, and I laugh as I walk away, intending to do just that.

"How was your run?" Dagan asks when Korbin and I come back into the house, both of us worn out. I look out the window to see it just start to pour down, and I'm damn thankful we got inside before that started.

"Good, but the more important question is whether or not those are waffles?" I ask, smelling them before I even get to his side and see the waffle maker he has out. I look over to the table, seeing cut fruit on a plate and all the sauces lined up. There are even plates and cutlery set out.

"Sit down, I've made you all some," he says, winking at me. The back door opens, and Eli walks in, the cigarette smoke clinging to his clothes letting me know what he was doing outside. He shakes his wet hair, before using his hand to push it out of his face. He takes his jacket off, resting it on a hook by the door.

"Morning," he says as I sit down, and Korbin hands me a bottle of orange juice before sitting next to me.

"Morning, cutie," I reply, seeing Eli narrow his eyes at me as Korbin laughs.

"Cutie?" he asks with a laugh, looking between us.

"Don't ask," I reply, and he chuckles. Eli sits down opposite me, still glaring and gently kicks my leg under the table, and I laugh. I pile some fruit on my plate, popping a strawberry in my mouth as Elias still looks annoyed.

"So . . . any plans after school today?" Korbin asks, cutting an apple up with a knife.

"I'm going to see Jules," I tell them.

"Want a ride?" Elias asks.

"Nope, Hallie is taking me as she wants to see her, too. They got along since Hallie was over here often. She wants to take her some grapes," I explain. Although she was only over here in memories Melody made up, they are real enough for Hallie. I doubt Hallie even remembers Melody now, it seems like no one really does. I haven't had to explain to any teachers where she is, Melody is so powerful she has messed with all their heads. Dagan slides the waffles onto my plate, and I grin up at him.

"Thank you," I say, and he puts another plate full of waffles in the middle of the table.

"Are you not serving mine up? I feel left out,"

Elias says, with a wounded, jokey expression as he pours maple syrup on my waffles. Dagan whacks him on the back of his head on the way back to his chair.

"When you're as pretty as Isola, then sure," he says, and Elias smirks, but doesn't reply as he starts pulling waffles onto his plate. I smile, looking at them all and enjoying how well we all just fit together like this. Having breakfast together, just relaxing together. It's so normal and perfect. I cut my waffles up, sticking a piece into my mouth, and try not to moan at how amazing it tastes. They must have cinnamon in them or something, because seriously, these waffles are better than any I've ever had.

"I'm kinda jealous of the waffles right now," Dagan comments, and I look up to see all the guys watching me, a mixture of amused and turned-on looks in their eyes.

"Why?" I ask, my voice muffled around my waffles. I'm not stopping eating to talk, this is too good.

"They make you smile more than anyone else," he says, and the guys all laugh.

"I was thinking they make you moan as much–" Elias starts to say, and Dagan leans over, whacking his head again.

"That hurts," Elias glares at his brother.

"Not as much as the stupid shit that comes out of your mouth does," he says, and I decide to intervene before the brothers start fighting and get in the way of me and my waffles.

"Yes, yes they do. My relationship with your cooking is becoming addictive, I may never let you out of my sight now," I joke, though he doesn't reply. We eat up, and when Dagan leans down to take my plate from me, he slants his lips close to my ear.

"Sounds good to me, kitty cat," he whispers and then walks off, leaving me with bright-red cheeks that I try to hide from the others, but they know and surprisingly, they don't say a word.

"Don't be silly, you look good," Hallie grins, and Jules laughs, waving a pale hand in the air. I spent the last hour brushing her hair, putting some dry shampoo in it for her, and then plaiting it. I couldn't stand to see her hair so messy, when she usually has it in a tight bun and styled, unless she has just gotten out of bed. Jules happily let me help her, and in some ways, it helped me feel better, too. I've been carrying so much guilt about not being able to look after her when I go back to Dragca, despite all the time she took care of me.

"I look awful. I have seen a mirror, little one," she replies to Hallie. Jules sits up a little in her bed, and pats the side next to her. Hallie goes to sit next

179

to her with a worried expression. I lean back in my seat, letting them have their moment alone together as I look out the window. Outside, rain is pouring down, hitting against the roof of the small side building of the hospital. It makes a soothing sound in the otherwise quiet room. I hate hospitals, it smells of death and loss in here. I can hear all the beeping machines trying to save people, and the cries of the families who lost someone close. It reminds me I haven't had time to truly grieve my father or Jace. I don't have somewhere to go to remember either of them. I try not to get lost in my own thoughts any more than I have to. I can't live in the past, with the people I had to leave behind there, there is only the future now.

"Come here, Isola?" she asks me. I get out of my chair and walk over, sitting on the edge of the bed, and holding her hand as Hallie gets up.

"I'm going to get us some drinks," Hallie says, patting my arm as she walks out of the room.

"You really don't look bad," I tell her, and she chuckles.

"And you have always been a terrible liar," she responds, making me smile because she has no idea that I lie to her all the time. That so much of my life is a lie, that there is little truth left here on Earth and in my life with Jules.

"You will be back home soon, I'm having to put up with Dagan cooking and takeaways. I miss you," I mumble out. Not that Dagan is bad at cooking, because he really, really isn't. But I'm not going to tell her that.

"I'm glad the boys are looking after you. They tell me you are well every time they come to visit me," she says, and I frown at her. *What boys?*

"They come to visit you? Elias, Dagan, and Korbin?" I inquire.

"Every day, one of the boys comes to see me," she explains, making me smile. They didn't have to do that, and I didn't even know they were. I love that Jules hasn't been as alone as I've worried she was. I wonder why they didn't tell me they were going to see her. They must have made a plan between them all or something.

"I haven't been able to email your father about being in here, have you spoken to him?" she asks. I close my eyes, looking away from her blue ones as I answer.

"No, I haven't. But I will," I say, hating that I'm lying again.

"Okay," she answers. "Isola, you can tell me

anything. You know that? I see you as the grandchild I never had," she says, and I look back, squeezing her hand tighter.

"I see you the same, but that's why I can't tell you everything. You are safe here and at the nursing home I chose for you until you are better," I say. She smiles, but there is an unspoken sadness clouding over her eyes. I want to tell her everything, but I doubt she would believe she has been raising a dragon her whole life. Nor that she has four living in her house right now.

"You will visit me?" she asks, her brown eyes watching me like it means everything to her for me to say yes.

"One day, when everything is settled, I will. I promise," I say, and I mean it. I will come back when I have the throne, and there is no war. When I can make her safe and maybe even bring her back to Dragca, show her my world. She could live out her days in the castle, with people to help her. I wonder if Bee could heal her a little, take away some of her pain.

"I know you lie to me all the time, and that you have your reasons. I know you're protecting me from something I don't need to know about. I'm just glad that sentence wasn't a lie, because I do want to see you at least one more time before I pass away," she says, and I frown.

"What—" I go to say when the door opens, and Hallie walks in. I pull my eyes away from Jules, intending to ask Hallie to give us some more time. I don't get the chance as Hallie starts talking quickly.

"I'm so sorry to cut this visit short. My father called, and I have to get back home. It's urgent," she says, putting the drinks on the side.

"Okay," I respond, seeing the worried look on my friend's face. I stand up, leaning over, and kissing Jules's forehead.

"I will see you soon, and we can discuss what you just said," I say, and she laughs.

"A lie, but I will always forgive you. It's what people do when they love someone," she replies, making me wonder if that's true. Hallie comes over before I can tell her she means a lot to me, too.

"I will come back on the weekend, and you can tell me that chocolate chip cookie recipe. I can't live without those in my life," Hallie says, making Jules laugh.

"I will write it down for when you come next, Hallie," Jules replies. Hallie gives her a hug before we both leave. I look back once more at Jules as I open the door, and she gives me a small nod. There is a look of love in her eyes that I know I won't forget. Yet, it's still hard to shut the door and walk out. I have a feeling I won't see her for a long time, and I hate it. It shouldn't be like this.

"What's so urgent with your dad?" I ask Hallie as we walk down the empty corridors of the hospital and neither of us have said a word.

"I can't really say, but something big has happened. He thinks I need to see it," she rolls her eyes.

"You confuse me," I bump her shoulder, "but I love you anyway."

"You best do, biatch," she grins, making me laugh.

TWENTY-TWO

"Hey, you're back, how was Jules?" Korbin asks as I close the door behind me, and start pulling my coat off, shaking the rain out of my hair. *Does it ever stop raining around here?*

"She is doing good. She is just wanting to get out of bed and start doing stuff," I say, pulling my boots off after hanging my coat up.

"Good to hear. We are watching a movie, and pizza is on the way. I've ordered your favourite: pepperoni and chicken," he says with a grin. He should know my favourite by now as we have all been taking turns ordering food for each other. I walk over, sliding my arms around his waist, and resting my head on his chest.

"Sounds perfect, and just what I need right now," I admit, and he kisses my forehead. Dagan walks down the stairs, stopping as he gets to us, and I let go of Korbin. It still feels a little awkward to hug or be close to any of them when there's another one of them around. Something to get used to, or not. *Who knows, they might suddenly change their minds and try to kill each other.*

"Welcome back," Dagan whispers, his fingers brushing my hand as he walks past me into the lounge.

"Go and sit down. I'll get you a drink," Korbin says, and walks off to the kitchen before I can reply to him. I walk into the lounge, loving how it's my favourite room in the house. It's the cosiest place in the house. It has three black-leather sofas, a fur rug on the floor in the middle, and they all face the stone fireplace. The television above the fireplace is on, and someone has lit the fire, so it's toasty warm in here.

"Come here," Dagan pats the space next to him on the sofa, and I go over to sit next to him. I rest my head on his shoulder as he flips through the movies on the Sky box.

"That movie looks good, I like end of the world

movies," I comment. I have a weird fascination with them.

"*San Andreas*?" he asks, and I nod.

"Okay, we have the movie picked then," he replies, renting it and pausing the movie when it starts up. Dagan holds me close to his side, seeming fascinated with twirling a strand of my blonde hair around his finger.

"Hey, princess," Elias says coming into the room. He puts his drink down near the sofa and sits down, stretching his legs out.

"How was school?" I ask him, just as the door-bell sounds. Elias and Dagan stare at each other, neither one of them moving to answer the door. I go to get up, myself, but Dagan's arm stops me.

"I'll get it then," Dagan says sarcastically, getting up and walking away. Elias grins, grabbing his drink, and moving to sit next to me.

"That's Dagan's seat," I laugh.

"I know, that was the plan. I miss you," he grins, wrapping an arm around my shoulder and pulling me to him. I laugh, snuggling into his side and not arguing, I'm sure Dagan won't be impressed when he gets back, but that's his argument to have.

"Asshole," Dagan grumbles when he walks in with the pizzas and sees Elias in his seat. Korbin walks in next, putting a glass of Coke on the floor for me and sitting down. Dagan passes the pizzas around to us, and I open mine up, inhaling the smell.

"Give it here, fucker," Elias grumbles as Dagan holds his box in the air, slowly opening the box.

"Nope," he says, and Elias gets up lazily, grabbing the pizza, but not stopping Dagan from grabbing a slice, which he shoves in his mouth.

"And they say *I'm* the asshole brother," Elias grumbles, moving back to his seat next to me.

"Damn, I love pizza, it's just amazing," I say, picking up one of my pieces and eating, okay inhaling, it in seconds. I look up to see all the guys looking at me, with matching smirks.

"I like a girl that loves her food," Elias grins as he picks the remote up and presses play. When I finish my pizza, I rest my head on Elias's shoulder and smile. This is a perfect moment, all of us here together, but it feels like I'm missing something. *Or someone.*

"Issy," Thorne's voice comes through the haze. I force my eyes open, but I can't see anything other than darkness.

It's an unsettling and scary darkness, one I just want to wake up from.

"Thorne? Where are you?" I ask nervously.

"Here," he says, and a hand grabs my arm. I turn, trying to see him, but I still can't, just a black shadow of a hand holding my arm.

"Why can't I see you?" I ask, feeling for his hand. It doesn't feel right, not solid but like air instead. It's so weird, and for some reason it scares me.

"I don't know why, but I think it's because we have been apart for too long," he tells me, his voice wavering at the end.

"Thorne," I mumble, wanting to tell him everything I learnt from Melody, but not like this, not when I can't even see his face.

"Your adoptive father killed my mother," I say, angry with him. Angry would be an understatement. I'm furious.

"Yes, but he was brainwashed into thinking your mother was evil, brainwashed into believing he was doing the right thing. It's no excuse, though, I don't blame you if you hate me for it," he says sadly.

"He still killed her, and you made me feel sorry for him and you!" I say, trying to move my arm away from him, but he doesn't let go.

"He did, hate me for that as well if you wish, just don't go," he whispers.

"Why do you want me to hate you?"

"Because I messed up, and I don't deserve forgiveness," he says, each word is more distant and faint than the next.

"Who brainwashed your father?" I ask quietly.

"I don't know, I never knew. My mother and I will kill whoever it was," he vows, but I can barely hear him.

"She doesn't know?" I ask, needing to know how much she has lied to him.

"No, she doesn't," he whispers.

"Stay safe, Isola, I don't think I'm strong enough to keep doing this," he says, and for some reason it makes me feel sick; the idea of never talking to him again, never seeing him again.

"You want to let me go, Thorne?" I ask.

"Never. I never want to let you go, but you should run from me," he whispers, and then everything goes black.

I BLINK MY EYES OPEN, hearing the television on in the background, and feeling my body resting on top of something hard and warm. I look down to see Elias underneath me on the sofa, my head on his chest, his heavy breathing tells me he is sleeping. I hear light snoring, and turn on my side to see Dagan sleeping on one of the sofas, and Korbin sleeping on the other. I slide off Elias slowly, careful not to wake him, and avoid the pizza boxes on the floor as I escape the room. I go through the kitchen and to the bathroom, turning the tap on and splashing my face with some water to wake me up. That dream was weird, and why am I suddenly so worried about Thorne? All I can think is that something is wrong, and there is nothing I can do. I'm tired of being here, helpless and not being able to do anything. I'm the princess of Dragca, the last ice royal, and my ancestors didn't back down. They didn't hide when everyone needed them, no, they went to war. They took the throne, demanded peace, and never let anyone beat them. The door opens behind me, snapping me out of my thoughts, and in the mirror, I see Dagan come in the room.

"Shit, sorry. I thought you had gone up to bed," he says. I shake my head, words escaping me as I still can't stop thinking about how much of a disappointment I am. How I'm meant to be making them remember me, instead I'm just falling for them. It's a massive cluster-fuck. I don't know if Dagan sees something written on my face, but he doesn't walk out, only holds the door as he looks at me like he can read my every thought.

"I only just woke up," I admit, and he shuts the door behind him. Dagan walks up to me, wrapping his arms around me from behind, and resting his head above mine. Our eyes meet in the mirror, neither of us looking away, and just finding some comfort and security in each other.

"Things are changing for us all, and it's getting complicated. Sure you don't want to run, kitty cat?" he asks, seductively in that panty-dropping voice that I swear these dragons have mastered. I could run from everything and live a life in hiding. But I would always be running once I started, and I would be heartbroken. I know I would, I couldn't leave them.

"I'm not running from anything anymore, especially not with how I feel. Life is so short, my life has taught me that, and it's pointless to fight what is right," I tell him, keeping my eyes locked with his. I want to make sure he understands every word. I will find a way to break the curse, to set them free and able to keep their dragons. Even if they don't want me in the end, even if I die making sure it happens, I'm going to do it.

"Tell me to stop, and I will," he says, as he tilts

my head to face him as he kisses me. The kiss is slow and leisurely as he holds me close to him. I moan as his hands tighten on my hips, sliding towards my stomach slowly. Every kiss teases me to the point of begging him. His right hand flicks open my jeans, as he slides his hand slowly into my jeans, and underneath my lacy underwear.

"You're a tease, Dagan," I moan, as his finger glides up and down my slit.

"I want to spend hours teasing you, learning your every reaction. What you like," he rubs a finger around my clit making me moan out in pleasure as he whispers, "what you love, and what makes you scream my name." He slowly slides one finger inside me, before taking it out and adding another.

"Watch me as I pleasure you, I want you to remember this," he demands, and I look at his eyes in the mirror, as he gets me closer and closer. So much passion, so much devotion is blazing in his eyes. He means every word, and I know after this, I will be his. I know I already was.

"Come for me, Isola, I want to see and feel you come," he whispers in my ear as his thumb finds my clit, and his masterful hands send me over the edge. I moan out, keeping my eyes locked with his—even though it's difficult—and my body pressed against his. He keeps his fingers inside me as I calm down, enough to tilt my head and look at him. I slide my hand to his belt, but he stops me with his other hand.

"No, beautiful," he whispers slowly, removing his fingers and stepping away. I watch breathlessly as he walks to the door.

"Don't you want to?" I ask.

"Not yet, there are plenty of things I want to do to you before I finally get to be inside you, kitty cat," he says with a seductive smirk, and walks out of the room.

TWENTY-THREE

"How was your exam?" Hallie asks, rubbing her forehead as we walk out of the dinner hall where we have been writing our exams for the last two hours. I didn't even see the point of trying to study for it, so I just drew the royal crest while I waited. I know I'm going to fail every class. The memories of being here for the last two years have nearly all gone, and all I remember are certain things, only the big things that happened. And that wasn't much, or anything to do with school.

"Shit, I know I failed it, but it doesn't really matter," I reply, and she sighs.

"You're lucky your parents aren't on your case

like mine. My dad would lose his shit if I failed," she says, and I reach over lifting a bit of her hair.

"Is that why you dyed the tips red?" I ask. I've never really known why she changes the colour.

"Yeah, I thought it would give me some confidence with the exam and dealing with my parents," she laughs sarcastically, "but it didn't."

"I'm sorry," I give her a side hug, trying to ignore the pangs of jealousy I feel. I wish my father was here to get angry that I didn't pass a test. That we could do simple things like that. Yet, even when he was alive, he didn't make much of an effort with normal things, because the crown came first. I remember reading a saying in a book once about becoming a queen or king. They say you give everything up for the crown, for the people you are chosen to rule. Maybe that was just the case with my father, he gave everything up in the end, even me.

"What happened yesterday after the hospital? You never said," I ask as we keep walking towards the front doors of the school.

"Nothing, he was just being overdramatic," she says, smiling tightly at me. I open the door, deciding not to call her out on lying to me. I really need to do some stalking of Hallie to find out what her father does. I literally have no idea from the clues she has given me. Something is going on, though, and I need to know what.

"Hey, princess, can I have a word?" Elias asks, leaning against a pillar, putting a cigarette out under his boot. *Does he ever stop smoking?*

"Have fun," Hallie winks, and walks off as I chuckle.

"What's up?" I ask him after I walk over. He looks down at me, his blue eyes sparkling and drawing me in.

"A date, we are going on a date," he announces.

"That doesn't sound like you're asking me," I raise an eyebrow. I don't like to be commanded to do anything.

"I'm not asking, you had one with Korbin, so I'm feeling left out," he says playfully, stepping closer, smoothing his hands down my arms.

"That's a shame, isn't it?" I tease. "If you ask nicely, I might go on a date with you," I say, making him laugh.

"Isola Dragice, will you go on a date with me?" he asks, somehow making the awkward question sexy. *Dammit.*

"Where did you have in mind?" I ask.

"Ice skating? Not what I expected," I say as we walk around the corner and stop in front of the ice skating building. It has ice boots glowing green next to a sign that says *"Skate for Ice."* A nice classic sign that I'm sure took someone hours to think up.

"You are an ice dragon, I'm pretty sure you like ice," he whispers next to my ear, his lips lightly grazing them.

"Okay, I'm an ice dragon that's never been ice skating," I admit, making him laugh. He tugs me towards the doors of the building. We walk in, get our boots after Elias pays, and go to sit on a bench to put them on. There aren't many people on the ice, or on the steps around it. It's a small ice ring, with plastic protectors and rails all the way around. The place looks like it could use some new paint, and overall is not in the best condition, but I bet it doesn't get a lot of visitors in this small town.

"Do you know how to skate?" I ask him, doing up the laces and pulling them tight. I stand up slowly, wobbling a little, even when I'm not on the ice. *This is not going to go well.*

"Maybe, I think so. I don't know, my memories are a little hazy," he says, getting confused because he doesn't remember what is real, and what is not. This is Melody's fake memories messing with him.

"Let's just go out, and see if you can," I say, and he stands up, not wobbling at all and reaches for my hand.

"Don't pull me over if you fall, princess," he requests, and I know if I fall, he is coming down with me. This was his idea, not mine.

"I promise I will," I say, grinning. I look away as we get to the ice, and let go of Elias to hold onto the rail. I slip straight away, grabbing the rail for dear life to make sure I don't fall over and hurt my ass.

"Princess, need a hand?" Elias says behind me, and I turn to see him skating around in circles. *Show off*. Of course he would be good at this.

"Nope," I bite out, determined to do this myself. I can make ice, so surely I can skate on it? Right?

"Ahh!" I scream as I fall over after letting go of the bars, smacking my right side on the freezing cold ice.

"I've got you, my stubborn pain in the ass," Elias says, picking me up and putting me on my feet like I weigh nothing. He holds me close to him, neither of us moving.

"I'm not stubborn," I point out, needing to say it.

"Yeah, princess, you are," he says, and then moves back a little, letting me grab his arms with my hands.

"Okay, come forward two steps, and then just glide. And repeat. It's easy, and I won't let go," he tells me, and I narrow my eyes at him.

"I'm not a kid," I say.

"Oh, I know," he says, his tone deeper and gruffer than before.

"Sorry, I just don't like not being able to do something," I tell him, taking two steps forward like he suggested and then letting the boots glide me along.

"Again," Elias says when I slow to a stop. I repeat the action, until I'm doing it without thinking, and we are skating around the ice together.

"Sometimes, you can't do everything alone. You need to accept help, in whatever forms it comes in," he tells me, and I know he is right. It's like going back to Dragca, I will need help. There is no way I will be able to win the throne back on my own. No, I have to start asking for help when I need it. Elias is right, but I'm not going to tell him that. His ego is big enough already.

"Even from the sexy biker man I'm on a date with?" I ask, and he pulls me to his chest, making me almost lose my footing as he holds me close to him.

"Even me," he whispers, and then kisses me.

TWENTY-FOUR

"Are you sure you don't want to come with us?" Korbin asks me, as he and Dagan pull their coats on. I lean against the wall, shaking my head.

"Nope, you need to do a food shop. I'm not going with you after last time," I shoot a pointed look at Dagan, who laughs.

"It wasn't that bad," he grumbles, walking out the door.

"It was! Watch out for the big pile of food this time!" I shout after him. Korbin chuckles and follows him out.

"Do you want anything special?" Elias asks as he comes out the kitchen and gets his coat.

"Chocolate, lots of chocolate."

"I should have known that answer," he grins. "What are you going to do today then?"

"I'm going to sit and read this book that came out today I've been waiting forever for!" I say excitedly, and he laughs, kissing my cheek before walking out and shutting the door. I grab my Kindle from my room, and run down the stairs, sitting on the sofa as I open a new book. I love the feeling when you start reading the first line of a new book and you know you are going to be hooked from just that one line. You also know you won't be putting it down for a long time. I settle down on the sofa just as my phone starts ringing.

"You have to be kidding me," I groan. I put the Kindle down and run into the kitchen, finding my mobile on the side. I just miss the call, but there are five messages from Hallie.

Hey! I decided to go to the party. Hot guy is going!
Okay, the party is boring.

I SKIM through the next couple of messages (who is hooking up with who at the party, and some girl was sick on a guy) to the last message.

Help me! I can't drive, and some guys won't leave me alone.

SHIT. I grab my coat, looking down at my leggings and green tunic top that stops at my knees. I don't look too bad, and she needs me; what I'm wearing isn't going to matter. I quickly call a local taxi firm and then wait outside, deciding not to call the guys. I'm stronger than they are right now anyway, and I can freeze anyone that touches Hallie. The taxi turns up ten minutes later as I keep calling Hallie's phone, and it goes straight to voicemail every time. I give the taxi driver Michael's address and sit back, still wondering if I should tell the guys. I quickly text Elias.

I'm going to Michael's party to pick Hallie up. Won't be long. X

I REST MY HEAD BACK, worrying more and more about Hallie. She takes self-defence like I do, and I remember her telling me her father taught her how to stop an attacker in seconds. She will be okay, she likely just needs a lift, and her phone is flat. Michael's house finally comes into view, a massive house in the middle of the woods on the other side of town. It must be five floors, with white panels and massive windows. There's loud music blasting from the house that I can hear from inside the car, even as we head up the driveway. There are students all over the lawn in front of the house, some making out, others smoking, and then I spot one student throwing up. *Gross.* I quickly pay the driver and get out, walking up the footpath and stepping over a passed-out guy in the middle of it.

"Issy!" I hear Michael shout my name from in front of me before I even get in the door. Michael jumps up from his seat in the living room I've walked into, like he was waiting for me or something. I look away, searching the room and seeing half of it is a smoky dance floor with loud music making it hard to hear anything, and sweaty teenagers dancing with each other all over it. The other half is full of sofas pushed together, teenagers all over them, doing things I quickly look away from when I don't see Hallie. *Shit, where is she?*

"I'm so glad you came!" Michael says, grabbing me and holding me tight to his sweaty and alcohol-stinking body.

"Have you seen Hallie?" I shout near his ear, smelling the beer and smoke on his clothes. He stinks so badly, and not in the good way.

"Upstairs, I will show you where she is. She is okay, don't worry, just a little drunk," he shouts back, taking my hand and pulling me through the people to another room with a large staircase. I don't trust when he says she is fine, but I don't have any choice but to let him lead me to where he said she is. He drags me up two floors, as we avoid drunk people on the stairs, and the sounds coming from the rooms.

"In this one, she was pretty drunk," Michael says, pointing at a door in the middle of three. I pull my hand away, walking over and opening it up. I walk in, seeing an empty bed and nothing else in the room. I turn as something sharp slips into my neck, and an arm wraps around my waist. Ice spreads down my hands as I try to fight the person holding me.

"Don't fight, little dragon, you're mine now," Michael whispers, licking my ear as everything goes black.

"Those look gross and seriously bad for you, man," I tell Dagan as he picks up his eighth packet of some tube of sweet powder things and chucks them into the trolley. I think I'm the only one that likes healthy food. Not pure sugar.

"I like sweet things," he winks at me, and I just groan, giving up on him. The whole trolley is full of crap, I know why Isola didn't want to come shopping with us now. I bet it took a year to put everything away.

"Come on, two trolleys full is enough," I say, staring as Dagan gets two more random sweet packets, and we walk to the next aisle where Elias is getting the last of the things on the list.

"Got everything?" I ask, seeing him searching his pockets.

"Yeah, I think," he says, "I just left my phone at home." He slips the note into his pocket and spins his trolley towards the other aisle. I'm half way down when I fall to my knees, screaming out from the pain and panic I feel. No, not that I feel, what Isola does. I can feel her, and she is in trouble. I go to open my eyes when a roar escapes my lips, and everything goes black as I hit the floor.

I BLINK MY EYES OPEN, *seeing another version of myself on the floor. I'm much younger, about ten, covered in mud as a man shouts at me. I don't know the man, yet I feel like I do. I can't look at this child version of me anymore, something makes me want to run away from it. I look away, at the ice behind me, so much ice.*

"Hello?" I ask, as a green little doll creature floats through the ice.

"She needs you. Save her, fire dragon. Save ice, save the light," the little doll says and suddenly a flash of memories hits me. Everything comes back. Isola. The throne. Dagan and Elias. My dragon.

"Save her," Bee pleads with me as I start falling, and I can't fight it.

. . .

"Kor, wake the fuck up," Elias's voice comes through the haze, and I feel a hand slapping the side of my face. "For fuck's sake."

I jump up when water is thrown over my face, and I wipe it away, looking around at the shopping aisles, to Elias standing over me with a bottle of water.

"Help me wake Dagan up, we have to find Isola. Something is wrong," Elias says, panic all over his face as he runs to his brother. I pull myself up, feeling for Isola, but not sensing anything. *How is that possible?*

"Get lost," Dagan grumbles as Elias shakes him. Elias starts pouring water over him when he doesn't wake up.

"Isola, wake up for Isola," Elias demands, and Dagan sits up, rubbing his face. My dragon pounds in my mind, its relief at finally being back clear.

"*Find princess, find mine,*" it hisses, trying to push me to shift in the middle of a store.

"Are you guys alright?" a woman asks, running down to us as Dagan gets up. I reach into my jeans and pull out my wallet.

"Can you put all this away for me? I'm so sorry,"

I say, as her eyes widen at the packed trolleys and then the wad of cash I get out, leaving it on top.

"Wait!" the woman shouts, but we all ignore her as we stumble out of the store and into the parking lot.

"We have to do what we were tasked with, we must protect Isola and get her to Dragca," Elias comments.

"The curse . . ." I let my sentence drift off and start pulling my coat off.

"We will pay the price," Elias says, but there's no hate in his words. We all shift, shooting off into the skies as we hear the screams from humans that see us.

"*Protect mine, and the curse will fall,*" my dragon says. He is prepared to lose himself for her. I know it.

"*I will lose you,*" I reply.

"*But you will have her, and she will be safe,*" my dragon whispers, and I know he is right. There isn't anything I wouldn't do to save her, and I've known that for quite some time.

TWENTY-SIX

ISOLA

Everything is blurry as I open my eyes. I feel cold, and someone is ripping something. A shadow is lying on top of me, pulling at my clothes, kissing my neck, and pushing their hardness into my stomach. Fear swallows me as I try to fight the darkness, I feel so out of sorts. Everything is cold again in a blink, and when I open my eyes, my surroundings are still so blurry that I can only make out shapes. Yet I can hear them, I feel the body moving off of mine.

"Shit, she is waking up and freezing stuff. You said that stuff knocks dragons out for a whole night!" I hear Michael shout at someone.

"Just be quick, and then I want my go before she really wakes up. My dad will lose his shit when he finds out I stole that stuff from the labs," the other guy says, in a whiny voice. Oh my god, I need to move, I can't let them do this to me. Fear strangles me as I try to do anything, only to fail, only to feel like I don't control my body.

"Shut up," I hear as I feel Michael pulling at my leggings. I try to move, to fight him as he pulls my underwear down, but I can't move. I can't do anything as I hear a belt being undone, every little sound making me utterly terrified. This is worse than dying, I would rather die than let him do this to me. I feel a tear slide down my cheek, the tear being the only thing I can focus on as I try to forget where I am. Panic, fear, and revulsion fill me as Michael spreads my legs and puts a knee on the bed, making the bed dip a little. I scream in my mind for my dragon, but I can't hear her. I can't do anything, and no one is coming to save me. The sound of a door slamming open fills the room, followed by the smell of smoke.

"You will die for this," Thorne's growly voice exclaims, but my mind refuses to believe it. He isn't really here. *He can't be.*

"It's not–" I hear Michael beg, and then he screams and screams. The smell of burning flesh fills the room as more screams follow Michael's. I try so

213

hard to move, to know if what I'm hearing is even real, to see anything other than the blurriness in front of me. The warmth of the fire in the room eventually takes over the sound of Michael's and the other's screams, and then something is wrapped around me.

"I know you hate me, but not like this, not before I can even tell you how much of a fucking idiot I am," Thorne whispers near me, and I feel hands on my face.

"I hate you," I mumble, trying to make the words ring true. I don't even know what I'm saying, I don't even believe it's really him.

"No, you don't, and you hate that," he says gently, and picks me up in his arms. I try to reply, but I can't, only seeing a shadow carrying me out of a fire. When Thorne's face comes into view, I can finally see the burning house just behind his head.

"You saved me, why?" I ask, feeling numb.

"Because in the end, I always will," he tells me, kissing the top of my head. I rest myself against him as I let darkness take me away.

TWENTY-SEVEN

"I didn't do a thing to her! I saved her, you fucking idiots!" I hear Thorne shout as I wake up. The memories of Michael and my resulting terror making me jump, and I fall off the sofa I'm on. I slam onto the wood floor, flinching at the coldness and how the room spins. I put a hand on my head, and I look around, somehow expecting him to be there, trying to force himself on me. I feel down my body, knowing I'm not in pain, so he couldn't have . . . . *I can't even say the word.*

"Shit," I hear Elias say, and then he is standing above me, leaning down to help me up. I grab the blanket, scooting away from him, and he holds his hands up.

"Hey, it's me, princess," he coaxes gently, not

taking another step closer. I look around the lounge, trying to relax now that I'm home and not in danger.

"I told you what happened, don't push her," Thorne says, coming to stand next to him.

"I remember, princess, we all do," Elias says gently.

"How?" I croak out, and clear my throat a few times. Dagan walks over, seeing me hiding in the corner of the sofa, and frowns. I look at the glass of water in his hand, but I don't really want him close enough to me to take it.

"Here, it's just water," he offers me the glass of water he was holding, reaching out, so he doesn't get too close. I accept it, and he backs away, sitting on the edge of the sofa. They all watch me with fear in their eyes, all of them look as worried as the next one. Elias and Thorne sit on the floor where they were, and it shocks me that they aren't arguing. Or not trying to kill each other.

"I got you some clothes," Korbin says as he walks in the room. He places them on the back of the sofa I'm hiding next to and then backs away, knowing I just don't want anyone near me right now. He sits by Dagan, all of them looking at me as I pull my blanket close around myself.

"How?" I repeat, needing to know what

happened to make them remember, and they all look at each other.

"We were shopping, just about to check out another aisle, when it happened. We felt your fear, your pain, and it overwhelmed us into remembering. We shifted outside and flew straight here just as Thorne carried you in and explained," Dagan explains. "I think we all passed out for a moment at the store."

"That's not possible, only mates or blood bound souls can feel each other's emotions in times of need," I point out, and they all look at each other.

"How do you know that?" Elias is the one to ask.

"Jace wanted to share blood with me before we mated, so he would know if I was in any danger. I decided I didn't want to, because I wanted our blood to be swapped at our mating," I explain, and there's an eerie silence between us all. They are hiding something from me, and I'm not sure I even want to know what it is they did.

"Tell me what you did, what you all did," I demand, knowing guilt when I see it in each of their eyes. I keep looking over at Thorne, not really believing that he is here.

"Wait, before you answer that, how are you here? How did you know?" I ask Thorne.

"I didn't know, but Melody must have as she came to me. She demanded I leave right then. She said she would meet us when we come back to Dragca," Thorne tells me, and I look down at the floor, taking a deep breath. I have to thank Melody and Thorne at some point.

"Is Michael . . .?" I stumble over his name, and I'm not sure Thorne even understood what I said until he answers.

"Dead." He says the word firmly, unapologetically, and full of protective tones. I clear my throat before looking at Dagan, and nodding for him to tell me what they all did.

"When you were stabbed, you were also poisoned and dying. Your uncle told us that you needed to have the poisoned blood taken out, and it had to be replaced," he says, his sentence drifting off as my eyes widen.

"You gave me blood to save me?" I ask.

"We all did, you needed a lot, and there was so much poison it was turning your blood black," he says, his haunted eyes communicating how horrible it was for him.

"We are blood bound, all of us?" I exclaim.

"Yes, we made the choice to die for you. We made the choice to give you our life then, because you are our queen. You are the one we fight for, and that hasn't changed in all the weeks we have been here," he says firmly.

"What has happened, the curse . . .?" I ask, and they look between each other.

"The curse doesn't work on Earth, but if we ever go back . . . we will lose them," Korbin says and then drifts off.

"I have to return, you don't," I tell them, and I mean every word. I might be their queen in their eyes, but I won't demand this of them.

"We do have to return home, and we made our choice a long time ago," Dagan says as Elias and Korbin nod. I look back at Thorne, and his next words crush my heart.

"My dragon is gone, it was the moment I made the choice to come here for you," he tells me, pain laced all over his face.

"Thorne . . ." I choke.

"Don't, it's done. Melody and Bee need you to get up, put your clothes on, and return home. They are waiting for you in Dragca," he says, and his firm words make me want to move.

"Don't let a stupid human win. You are Isola Dragice, and you don't give up," Thorne tells me. I close my eyes, calling my dragon.

"*Will you fight with me? Are you ready for this?*" I ask her.

"*I am with you, always,*" she replies.

"*It's time to go home,*" I whisper a reply and open my eyes, knowing they are silver as I stare at all my dragon guards.

Home to fight and win.

TWENTY-EIGHT

"Who are you calling?" Thorne asks me as we walk through the woods and to the nearest portal.

"My friend, Hallie. I can't just vanish from her life," I say as I ring her house phone, knowing Michael must have stolen Hallie's cell, and he nods. I doubt Hallie was even at the party, and the more I think about it, I was stupid to fall for that trick.

"Maybe you can tell me about her one day?" he asks and every instinct in me wants to say no, while other parts just want to run to him. Let him hold me, and tell me everything's okay. I don't know why I feel so safe with him, whether it's because he saved me, or if it's because we share a blood bond. I don't know, but it's hard to resist the pull. It also makes sense how he was getting in my dreams now, even across worlds. If our connection is so strong already, I don't even want to think about how powerful it could be if we mated. Not that I'm thinking about mating. *Not at all.*

"Maybe," I say quietly as the phone rings and rings, finally going to voicemail. I wait for the beep before I start talking, and I see Elias look over to me as he speaks quietly to Korbin and Dagan to my left.

"Hallie, this isn't going to make much—or really any—sense. But here we go. I have to leave, for a long time, and I have no idea when I can come back. Jules has a nursing home set up, and she knows where the cash is in the house, but can you please check on her?

"Also, I never had a best friend, or anyone that close to me, but you are that to me and that will never change. I love you, Hallie, and stay safe for me." I go to say more when it starts beeping, and I know I have to put the phone down.

I wipe some stray tears away, and even though Thorne doesn't look my way, he says quietly, "I will make sure you see her and Jules again, this isn't the end." I don't reply to him, I can't tell him how much comfort I received from his words. We walk silently to the portal, seeing the shimmer in the trees in the dim morning light.

"You don't have to come; in fact, I won't allow it. I can't let you give your dragons up for me," I stop in front of the portal, turning to my dragon guards. If they walk through this portal, they won't be dragons anymore, just guards. It won't change how I feel for them, but it might change how they feel about me. I still shake a little when they move near me, even though I know they would never hurt me like Michael tried to. I have to close my eyes, and force myself to push what happened into a little box in the back of my head. I can't cope with it right now. *I just can't, more urgent things are going on.* Thorne nods sadly, walking to the portal, whispering where we need to go, and giving us some alone time.

"We all knew what we were doing when we gave you our blood," Dagan says.

"But the last few weeks, I did this. You didn't know who you were, what you were!" I exclaim.

"You did try to tell us, princess," Elias replies.

"It doesn't matter, I did this. I caused this," I say, getting more and more upset.

"Isola . . . just trust us. There are things we need to tell you, things that will make you understand,"

Dagan says, keeping an eye out for anyone around us. Not that there will be anyone, we are in the middle of the woods.

"Then tell me?" I ask them all. "I can't believe that you would choose this."

"It's my choice, princess. I told you once already . . . I've made my mind up about you, and I never lie," Elias says with a smirk, but I see the fear flash over his eyes. He doesn't want to lose his dragon, and yet he is still going to walk into Dragca for me. I watch as he walks past me and straight into the portal without stopping once. Thorne nods once at me before following him, and there is a long silence between us all.

"I do have to come with you, I'm yours. I don't need to tell you anything else, doll," Korbin smirks. I can see his fear, too, but like Elias, he walks past me and into the portal. My heart pounds against my chest as Dagan steps closer to me, placing his hands on my face.

"Stay here, please don't do this," I beg him, not wanting him to lose that part of himself. I can't bear for the curse to destroy that part of him.

"Isola, stop it," he demands as I try to move away from him.

"No, this is crazy, what you're saying and going

to do . . . It can't," I mumble and then trail off when his dragon takes over, the blackness burning over his eyes. I stumble away from him, walking backwards towards the portal.

"Stop!" he shouts and storms over to me, pinning me to a tree, and levelling his eyes with mine, so I can't look away.

"If it's a choice between my dragon, a part of my soul, and you, I. Choose. You." he says, growling out all his words.

"Dagan," I whisper.

"It would crush me more to lose you. *That* would destroy my soul more than anything any curse can do to me. My dragon agrees because, you know what?" he asks. I shake my head.

"He would die for you," he tells me, kissing me gently and stepping back. He walks through the portal as tears stream down my face. The curse meant to protect me is destroying the only things I care about. I step forward, closing my eyes, and walking through the portal as I hear whispered by the sweetest voice:

"The last light returns, and the darkness will be stopped."

TWENTY-NINE

The portal lets me out on the other side, and the bright light from the suns blinds me for a little bit, until I can open my eyes and see what's in front of me. Elias, Dagan, and Thorne are standing to one side, and Korbin is right in front of me, with a long red sword resting under his chin. A tiny amount of blood is dripping down his neck. I follow the sword to see Esmeralda holding it, a smug smile on her painted red lips that match her red cloak. Guards come from all directions to surround us, raising their swords that shine in the sunlight. I know she has won, I can't do anything other than lower my hands. She would kill Korbin in a second because he means nothing to her, and I won't let her kill anyone else I care about again.

"You are all coming to the castle, and then meeting your *true* fate," she glances at Thorne, "even you, who dares to betray his mother for a stupid girl."

"Not a girl, a queen. I didn't betray my mother, I'm putting right the mistakes we have made. The throne isn't ours, and my mother is going mad from the power!" he shouts at her, and she shakes her head.

"So, so disappointing," she tuts.

"No, that would be you. You should really tell your dear sister where you go next time, Esmeralda, and maybe get some more guards," Melody's voice comes from above us, and I look up just as she jumps down, slamming Esmeralda to the ground. Korbin grabs her sword, as Esmeralda throws Melody off her. From the corner of my eye, I see Elias slam a hand into his guard, grabbing his sword and running it through the guard's stomach. Korbin runs to help them just as all hell breaks loose, and my dragon guard make quick work of killing the guards surrounding us.

"Are you going to fight me fairly, princess?"

Esmeralda taunts. "Or die quietly, in shock, just like your pretty ice dragon and dead daddy did."

"You never played fair, and neither will I," I say, stepping forward. I raise my hands out in front of me, making a long Bo-shaped ice staff, with deadly spikes on either end. Esmeralda doesn't wait for more than a second, shooting three arrow-shaped fire sticks at me. I raise my staff, hitting each one as I walk slowly towards her. She shoots more and more, until I can't see her over the fire in front of me, until I'm standing right in front of her. I whack her legs out from under her, holding the spike at the bottom of the staff right above her heart.

"Don't even think about it," I say, leaning down as she looks up at me with fear-filled eyes.

"You . . . will . . . regret . . . this," she whispers each word as I lift the staff and slam it into her heart, without a second thought. Her eyes widen, her lips parting as blood drips down the side of her face.

"That is for Jace, you goddamn bitch," I say, making sure she hears every word before letting go of the staff. I look around, seeing the guys still fighting three guards. I make three ice spikes, spinning around and throwing them at each guard using my dragon's eyesight, pinning them to the trees with the spike in the middle of their stomachs. Thorne and Korbin run to my sides, protecting me even though there is no one left to hurt me now. I run to Melody, shaking her a little, and she groggily wakes up, holding a hand to the back of her head. I help her sit up as Elias and Dagan get to us, surrounding Melody and me.

"You did it, sis," she says, pulling me to her and holding me tight.

"Sister? What did we miss?" I hear the guys talking and remember I never told them. I hear her sharp intake of breath from Melody before she pulls back. I follow her gaze to Esmeralda's body.

"We have to leave, you shouldn't have killed her. I see her alive no matter what you did here," Melody tells me, pulling my arm, and I look away from Esmeralda to see the desperation in her eyes.

"The future is changing, and it's darker than ever. That's why we are here. We must run before she gets here, the light must live," a small voice says, a green head of hair popping out of Melody's cloak.

"Bee," I shout, as she flies to me, landing on my hand. She is bigger and brighter, her skin almost glows now. I feel so relieved to see her, to have her close to me. "I missed you, I thought I'd never get to see you again."

"Stop darkness, light must win. We *must* win," she demands, her voice older and far more serious than she has ever been. I lower my hand as Bee flies to my shoulder, holding onto my hair as I stand up. Melody stands with me, and we look around at all the bodies. So much death.

"I made a vow, and I won't regret it," I tell Melody.

"Death always comes with a price," she says, nodding her head to the left of me. I look around to see Melody's face full of worry, Elias wiping blood off a sword, Dagan staring at the ice. That is until I see Thorne, who is just staring at the body of his aunt. I killed his aunt. Our families . . . we have all killed so much of each other. With so much death, can there be anything left but hate? Or just pain. I still walk over to him, softly placing my hand on his arm, making him flinch, but he doesn't move away.

"I'm sorry, I know she is family," I whisper.

"She wasn't family, not after the choices she made and the deaths she caused. You have no idea the amount of destruction she has caused in Dragca since you have been gone," Thorne snaps out, walking away from me. I go to follow him when I hear a pained grunt.

"Issy," Korbin whispers, and then falls to the

ground as I turn to look at him. I drop down next to him as the others run over, and I look to where he is holding a hand against his shirt, and it's bleeding. I lift it up, seeing a deep cut, with purple lines spreading out from it slowly. I panic, pulling my hoodie off and pressing it against the cut.

"I'm going to be fine," Korbin says, but any fool could hear the pain in his voice.

"Don't lie," I say, and he holds my hand, squeezing it tightly.

"Here, out of the way," Dagan says, kneeling next to me.

"I'm going to burn the cut, seal it and stop it bleeding. It's the best we can do until we find some-where to go," Dagan explains, moving my hoodie off the long cut.

"Do you even have your fire still? Without your dragon?"

"I can't hear my dragon anymore, but yes," Dagan says, holding out a small flame in his hand. "Only I can't do it for long. Nothing like the power I used to have."

"You can't do that," I say and look to Bee. "Can you heal him?"

"Not from poison, not without power," she says sadly, and my dragon growls, whines, and demands I do something in my mind. Anything to save him.

"Look away," Korbin demands of me, and Elias pulls me away, turning my head into his chest as I hear Korbin scream and scream. I don't think I will ever forget the sounds of his screams, I don't want to. It reminds me that I could lose him, it reminds me what I need to fight for. When it stops, I fall to Korbin's side next to Dagan. I examine the cut, it's burnt and no longer bleeding, but the purple lines look darker and longer.

"I'm okay, don't worry, doll," he tries to reassure me, reaching up and wiping some of my tears away.

"He is poisoned, we need to find a town, and a healer quickly," Melody says nervously, looking over my shoulder.

"Can you walk?" I ask Korbin, and he shakes his head with a tired look. Elias and Dagan lift him up, keeping an arm around their shoulders. But I know he won't be walking fast.

"*Save mine,*" my dragon whimpers, before disappearing away in my head.

"What is the nearest town? Where do we go now?" I ask, but I don't really know who I'm asking. I don't know where we are, it's just trees and mountains for a long time.

"To the seers near here, we have to show them you're alive. To show that you want to fight, and hope they will let their healers save him," Melody says.

"We have allies here, things you don't know, Issy. We have a lot to tell you," Dagan comments.

"I could fly ahead and get help," I suggest.

"No flying, they will be looking for an ice dragon in the skies, and the reward on your head is high. Poor people do desperate things, and we will be lucky if they even help you save your guard," Melody says.

"Let's go now. They *will* save him, or I will kill anyone who thinks to let him die," I promise, turning around. Looking once more at the ice staff melting into Esmeralda's body, I wipe a tear away. *Jace finally has his justice, but why do I feel like I just made a huge mistake, a mistake that could cause me to lose everything that is alive, for a promise I made to death?*

EPILOGUE
TATARINA

"There are rumours the king was seen this way with the princess and other guards," one of the royal guard says, a nervous look flitting across his young face as he stares at me. I smile, placing my hand on his shoulder and feel him shaking. I laugh, and walk around him in the direction he pointed at. I can't believe my son would betray me, not for that spoilt princess. He wouldn't do that to me.

"Your highness, we have located your sister," a guard says running over to me breathlessly, placing an arm out in front of me to stop me from seeing what is behind him. Like I need to be hidden from the darkness that is this night. I lift a hand, a hot breeze of fire whacks into him, and sends him flying out of my way. I stop, staring at the bodies littering the ground and the one right in the middle.

"NO!" I scream, running over to my sister, dropping down to my knees at her side. There's a hole in her chest, blood surrounds her which mixes in with her long red hair. Too much blood, and it's too watered down. Someone used ice here. My beautiful sister is lost. *Who could have done this?*

"Queen," a hushed voice says, making me look up as a dark shadow hovers above us. My dark spirit, Nane, flies out the shadow, floating down to me.

"Nane, she is dead," I say, refusing to cry. I haven't cried for many years, and I won't now. I will get revenge, I will destroy this world for what it has always done . . . taken everything from me.

"The light killed her, the light must pay," she whispers to me, and lands on the stomach of Esmeralda, lifting a blood-covered hand. "Blood and ice."

"Isola? She did this?" I question Nane, who nods, and I close my eyes as a scream leaves my lips. Black shadows spread out from under me, going in every direction and burning away the trees near me as I try to reel in my anger. They burn the guards, and I hear them, their screams are almost pleasurable to hear. Someone has to suffer for this, for my sister.

"I. Will. Kill. Her," I bite out as I open my eyes

and lean forward, tucking a lock of Esmeralda's red hair behind her ear. *My sweet little sister.*

"We can bring her back, bring her back stronger than ever. Bring her back linked to your life, and she will never leave you," Nane suggests, looking up at me with a wicked grin.

"Will she be the same?" I ask.

"She will have a dark soul, much like yours," Nane says, and I laugh.

"She had one before death, but now she will want revenge," I say, a large smile playing on my lips as I place both my hands on Esmeralda's head.

"Call darkness," Nane whispers, and sends a blast of darkness straight into me through our bond. Black lines spread down my arms, onto my sister's face. They crawl up her face slowly and painfully for me. When they hit her eyes, I pull back, catching a breath, and stand up. I wait for a long time, knowing it takes a while for a body to come back. Finally, Esmeralda's eyes open slowly. She looks up at me as I stand over her, her eyes blood red, and a sinister grin on her lips as she stands with my help.

"Time to hunt a princess, my sister," she says, her voice darker and almost sweet. Like a sweet berry that you don't know will kill you, until you're dead.

"Then let's hunt," I say, and Nane laughs as she floats into the shadows once more, but I hear her dark whisper in my mind.

"Darkness will win; not only Dragca will fall, but Earth, too ..."

The End

Wings of Spirit link here (Protected by Dragons book three).

About G. Bailey

G. Bailey is a USA Today and international bestselling author of books that are filled with everything from dragons to pirates. Plus, fantasy worlds and breath-taking adventures.
G. Bailey is from the very rainy U.K. where she lives with her husband, two children, three cheeky dogs and one cat who rules them all.

(You can find exclusive teasers, random giveaways and sneak peeks of new books on the way in Bailey's Pack on Facebook or on TIKTOK— gbaileybooks)

Find more books by G. Bailey on Amazon...

Link here.

PART ONE
BONUS READ OF
THE MISSING WOLF

I'm Anastasia Noble, and shortly after moving to college, my life changed forever.

I became a familiar, bonded to a wolf for life and arrested simply for existing.

I woke up in the famous Familiar Empire community where I have to learn to bond with my wolf, or I can never leave.

Never again see those whom I love.

Bonding is my only option, if you could even call it an option, but add in familiars going missing every week, plus being stuck in a cabin with three mysterious, attractive, male familiars and their maddening animals...*this is not going to be easy.*

17+ RH

THE MISSING WOLF

LEAVING THE PAST BEHIND.

ANASTASIA

I stand still on the side of the train tracks, letting the cold wind blow my blonde and purple dip-dyed hair across my face. I squeeze the handle of my suitcase tighter, hoping that the train will come soon. *It's freezing today, and my coat is packed away in the suitcase, dammit.* I feel like I've waited for this day for years, the day I get to leave my foster home and join my sister at college. I look behind me into the parking lot, seeing my younger sister stood watching me go, my foster grandmother holding her hand. Phoebe is only eleven years old, but she is acting strong today, no matter how much she wants me to stay. I smile at her, trying to ignore how difficult it feels to leave her here, but I know she couldn't be in a better home. I can get through college with our older sister and then get a job in the city, while living all together. *That's the plan anyway.*

We lost our mum and dad in a car accident ten years ago, and we were more than lucky to find a foster parent that would take all three of us in. Grandma Pops is a special kind of lady. She is kind and loves to cook, and the money she gets from fostering pays for her house. She lost her two children in a fire years ago, and she tells us regularly that we keep her happy and alive. Even if we do eat a lot for three kids. Luckily, she likes to look after us as I burn everything I attempt to cook. And I don't even want to remember the time I tried to wash my clothes, which ended in disaster.

"Train four-one-nine to Liverpool is calling at the station in one minute," the man announces over the loudspeaker, just before I hear the sound of the train coming in from a distance. I turn back to see the grey train speeding towards us, only slowing down when it gets close, but I still have to walk to get to the end carriage. I wait for the two men in front of me to get on before I step onto the carriage, turning to pull my suitcase on. I search through the full seats until I find an empty one near the back, next to a window. I have to make sure it's facing the way the train is going as it freaks me out to sit the other way. I slide my suitcase under the seat before sitting down, leaving my handbag on the small table in front of me.

I wave goodbye to my sister, who waves back, her head hidden on grandma's shoulder as she cries. I can only see her waist length, wavy blonde hair before the train pulls away. I'm going to miss her. *Urgh, it's not like we don't have phones and FaceTime!* I'm being silly. I pull my phone out of my bag and quickly send a message to my older sis, letting her know I am on the train. I also send a message to Phoebe, telling her how much I love and miss her already.

"Ticket?" the train employee guy asks, making me jump out of my skin, and my phone falls on the floor.

"Sorry! I'm always dropping stuff," I say, and the man just stares at me with a serious expression, still holding his hand out. His uniform is crisply ironed, and his hair is combed to the left without a single hair out of place. I roll my eyes and pull my bag open, pulling out my ticket and handing it to him. After he checks it for about a minute, he scribbles on it before handing it back to me. I've never understood why they bother drawing on the tickets when the machines check the tickets at the other end anyway. I put my ticket back into my bag before sliding it under the seat just as the train moves, jolting me a little.

I reach for my phone, which is stuck to some paper underneath it. I've always been taught to pick up rubbish, so I grab the paper as well as my phone before slipping out from under the table and back to my seat. I put my phone back into my handbag before looking at the leaflet I've picked up. It's one of those warning leaflets about familiars and how it is illegal to hide one. The leaflet has a giant lion symbol at the top and warning signs around the edges. It explains that you have to call the police and report them if you find one.

Familiars account for 0.003 percent of the human race, though many say they are nothing like humans and don't like to count them as such. Familiars randomly started appearing about fifty years ago, or at least publicly they did. A lot of people believe they just kept themselves hidden before that. The Familiar Empire was soon set up, and it is the only place safe for familiars to live in peace. They have their own laws, an alliance with humans, and their own land in Scotland, Spain and North America.

Unfortunately, anyone could suddenly become a familiar, and you wouldn't know until one random day. It can be anything from a car crash to simply waking up that sets off the gene, but once a familiar, always a familiar. They have the mark on their hand, a glowing tattoo of whatever animal is bonded to them. The animals are the main reason familiars are so dangerous. They have a bond with one animal who would do anything for them. Even kill. And I heard once that some kid's animal was a lion as big as an elephant. But those are just the things we know publicly, who knows what is hidden behind the giant walls of the Familiar Empire?

"My uncle is one, you know?" a girl says, and I look up to see a young girl about ten years old hanging over her seat, her head tilted to the side as she stares at the leaflet in my hand. "He has a big rabbit for a familiar."

"That's awesome..." I say, smiling as I put the leaflet down. I bet picking up giant rabbit poo isn't that awesome, but I don't tell her that.

"I want to be a familiar when I grow up," she

excitedly says. "They have cool powers and pets! Mum won't even let me get a dog!"

"Sit down, Clara! Stop talking to strangers!" her mum says, tugging the girl's arm, and she sits down after flashing me a cheeky grin.

I fold the leaflet and slide it into my bag before resting back in the seat, watching the city flash by from the window. I couldn't think of anything worse than being a familiar. You have to leave your family, your whole life, and live in the woods. *Being a familiar seems like nothing but a curse.*

Keep reading here...

THE MISSING WOLF

WHO WEARS A CLOAK THESE DAYS?

"Ana!!" my sister practically screeches as I step off the train, and then throws herself at me before I get a second to really look at her. Even though my sister is only a few inches taller than my five-foot-four self, she nearly knocks me over. I pull her blonde hair away from my face as it tries to suffocate me before she thankfully pulls away. I'm not a hugger, but Bethany always ignores that little fact.

"I missed you too, Bethany," I mutter, and she grins at me. Bethany was always the beautiful sister, and as we got older, she just got prettier. Seems the year at college has only added to that. Her blonde hair is almost white, falling in perfect waves down her back. Mine is the same, but I dyed the ends a deep purple. Another one of my attempts at sticking out in a crowd when I usually become invisible next to my gorgeous sister. Phoebe is the image of Bethany, and both of them look like photos of our mother. Whereas I look like my dad mostly, I still have the blonde hair. Bethany grins at me, then slowly runs her eyes over my outfit before letting out a long sigh.

"You look so pretty, sis," she says, and I roll my eyes. Bethany hates jeans and long-sleeved tops, which I happen to be wearing both. I didn't even look at what I threw on this morning. I shiver as the cold wind blows around me, reminding me that I should have gotten my coat out my suitcase on the train trip. It is autumn.

"You're such a bad liar," I reply, arching an eyebrow at her, and she laughs.

"Well, you are eighteen now, and I've never seen you in a dress. College is going to change all that." She waves a hand like she has sorted all the problems out.

"How so? I'm not wearing a dress to classes," I say, frowning at her. "Leggings are much easier to run around in, I think."

"Parties, of course," she tuts, laughing like it

should be obvious. Bethany grabs hold of my suit-case before walking down the now empty sidewalk to the parking lot at the end.

"I need to study. There is no way I'm going to ace my nursing classes without a lot of studying," I tell her. Bethany took drama, and I wasn't the least bit surprised when she was offered a job at the end of her course, depending on her grades. Though she was an A-star student throughout high school, so there is no way she could fail.

"I love that you will have the same job mum did," she eventually tells me, and I glance over at her as she smiles sadly at me before focusing back on where she is walking. I remember my mum and dad, whereas Bethany is just over one year older than me and remembers a lot more. Phoebe doesn't remember them at all; she only has our photos and the things we can tell her. It was difficult for Bethany to leave us both to come to college, but grandma and I told her she had to find a future.

"I doubt I will do it as well as her...but I like to help people. I know this is the right thing for me to do," I reply, and I see her nod in the corner of my eye. I quickly walk forward and hold the metal gate to the car park open for Bethany to walk through before catching up with her as we walk past cars.

"You've always been the nice one. I remember when you were twelve, and the boy down the road broke up with you because some other girl asked him out. The next day, that boy fell off his bike, cutting all his leg just outside our home. You helped him into the house, put plasters on his leg, and then walked his bike back to his house for him," she remarks. "Most people wouldn't have done that. I would have just laughed at him before leaving him on the sidewalk."

"I also called him a dumbass," I say, laughing at the memory of his shocked face. "So I wasn't all that nice."

"That's why you are so amazing, sis," she laughs, and I chuckle as we get to Bethany's car. It's a run down, black Ford Fiesta, but I know Bethany adores the old thing. Even if there are scratches and bumps all over the poor car from Bethany's terrible driving.

"Get in, I can put the suitcase in the boot," she says, and I pull the passenger door open before sliding inside. I do my seatbelt up before resting back, watching out of the passenger window at the train pulling out of the station. There is a man in a black cloak stood still in the middle of the path, the wind pushing his cloak around his legs, but his hood is up, covering his face. I just stare, feeling stranger and more freaked out by the second as the man lifts his head. I see a flash of yellow under his hood for a brief moment, and I sit forward, trying to see more of the strange man I can't pull my eyes from. I almost jump out of my skin when Bethany gets in the car, slamming her door shut behind her, and I look over at her.

"Are you okay? You look pale," she asks, reaching over to put her hand on my head to check my temperature before pulling it away. I look back towards the man, seeing that he and the train are gone. Everything is quiet, still and creepy. *Time to go.*

"Yeah, everything is fine. I'm just nervous about my first day," I tell her, which is sort of honest, but I'm missing the little fact about the weird hooded man. *I mean, who walks around in cloaks like friggin' Darth Vader?* She frowns at me, seeing through my lies easily, but after I don't say a word for a while, she drops it.

"It will be fine. Don't worry!" she says, reaching over to squeeze my hand before starting the car. I keep my eyes on the spot the man was in until I can't see it anymore. I close my eyes and shake my head, knowing it was just a creepy guy, and I need to forget it. This is my first day of my new life, and nothing is going to ruin that.

THE MISSING WOLF

ONE MOMENT CAN CHANGE EVERYTHING.

"Anastasia Noble?" I hear someone shout out as I wait in the middle of the crowd of new students. Bethany left me here about half an hour ago, and she is going to find me later once I have my room sorted. First, I have to get through a tour of the university, even though I had a tour here when I visited two months ago. I also spent days studying the map they gave me, so I know where I am going. Putting my hand in the air, I move through the crowd, pulling my suitcase behind me with my arm starting to ache from lugging the giant purple suitcase everywhere.

I get to the front of the crowd, where an older man waves me over. I quickly make my way to him and the three other students waiting at his side. Two of them are girls, both blonde and whispering between themselves with their pink suitcases. The other is a guy who is too interested in ogling the blondes to notice me coming over. Story of my life right there. I stop right in front of the older man who stinks of too much cologne, and I shake his slightly sweaty hand before stepping back.

"Welcome to Liverpool University. We are the smallest, but fiercest, university in northern England. Now, I am going to show you around the basic area before taking you to your rooms. You all will share a corridor and living area, so look around at your new friends and maybe say hello!" the man says, clapping his hands together before quickly turning to walk away. We all jog to catch up with him as he walks us across the grass towards one of the buildings on either side of the clearing.

There is a little river in the middle with planted flowers and trees all surrounding it. It's peaceful, exactly why my sister chose this university, I suspect. She always likes seeing the beauty in life, where I am always looking for a way to fix the world instead. I wish we had other family around that could tell us about what our parents were like, who each of us follow, or if we are just random in the family line of personalities. We don't even know if our parents had any close friends. There is nothing much in our foster pack given to grandma from social services. Bethany and I talked about going to the village we lived in to ask around, but neither of us ever found the time.

"Anastasia, right?" a guy asks, slowing down to walk at my side. He has messy brown hair, blue eyes, and a big rucksack on his back.

"Yep, who are you?" I ask.

"Don. Nice to meet you," he replies, offering me a hand to shake with a big grin. I shake his hand before looking up at the massive archway we are walking through to get inside of the building. It is two smooth pillars meeting together in the middle. There are old gargoyle statues lining the archway, their creepy eyes staring down at me. Those statues always creep me out. Bethany thinks it's funny, so last Christmas, she got me gargoyle romance books as a joke. Jokes on her though; some of those books were damn good. I quickly look away, back to where we are walking, as Don starts talking again.

"I've heard there is a party tonight to welcome freshers. Are you going?" he asks me, his arm annoyingly brushing against mine with how closely he has decided to walk. I glance up at him to see his gaze is firmly focused on my breasts rather than my face.

"No. I need to unpack," I curtly reply.

"Can't it wait one night?" he asks, and I look over at him once again. He is gorgeous, but the whiney attitude about a party is a big turn off. "I will make sure you have fun."

"No. It can't wait, and I doubt anything you could do would make the party fun for me," I say honestly, and not shockingly, he nods before catching up with the two blonde girls in the group, trying his pickup techniques on them. *Men.*

Bethany says I'm picky, but actually, it's just because the general male population at my age are idiots and act like kids most of the time too. I don't see how anyone could want to date them, though Bethany is on her twelfth boyfriend since she came to college, so I know she doesn't share my opinion. She swears she will know when the right guy comes along, and it will be the same for me. I doubt it. Anyway, finding the "right" guy is not the most important thing at the moment; passing college and getting my nursing degree is.

"This is the oldest part of the university and where most the lessons are. In the welcome packs sent to your old homes were the links to an app which is a map. It will help you find your lessons," the tour guide explains before opening a door out of the old corridor and into another one which is more modern. There are white-tiled floors, lockers lining the walls, and spotlights in the ceiling that shine so brightly everything gleams. "Every student gets a locker here, which is perfect for storing books and anything you don't need for every class. Trust me, you will get a lot of books, so the lockers are a godsend."

We walk down the corridor, listening to the guide explain the history of the university when suddenly there is a burning feeling in my hand that comes out of nowhere. I scream, dropping to my knees as I grab my hand, trying to stop the incredible pain. I rub at my pale skin as it burns hot, yet there is nothing there to see. The pain gets worse until I can't see or hear anything for a moment, and I fall back. When I blink my eyes open, I'm lying on the cold floor, hearing the chatter of students near me. No one is helping me, oddly enough, and they sound like they are far away. Every part of my body hurts, aches like I've been running a marathon.

"She's a familiar. Has anyone called the police?" one person asks as I stare up at the flickering spotlight right above me.

"We should leave; she could hurt us. Who knows where her creature is!" another man harshly whispers. I lift my hand above my face almost in slow motion. My eyes widen in pure shock at the huge, glowing, purple wolf tattoo covering the back of my hand where it burned. It stops at my wrist, the wolf's fur extending halfway up my fingers and thumb. The eyes of the wolf tattoo glow the brightest as I realise what this means.

"I'm a familiar."

THE MISSING WOLF

TIME TO RUN BEFORE IT IS TOO LATE.

As soon as I've said it out loud, it feels like I can't breathe as I sit up and look around at the people staring at me. The group I was with are huddled by the lockers a good distance away from me now, and I turn to see more people have shown up, a few of them on their phones. All of them are scared, worried what I will do as they keep their eyes on me. They are going to call the police and have me taken away because of this. *I have to get to Bethany first.* I have to at least say goodbye to her before they come for me and take me some place where I may never see her again.

I quickly scramble to my feet and run down the corridor, passing everyone who shouts for me to stop, until I get to the door at the end. I push it open, running through the arch and into the empty clearing. Stopping by the river, I look up and quickly try to remember how to get to the dorms. Shit, I don't even know what room she is in. I pull my handbag off my shoulder to get my phone out just as I hear a low growl from right behind me.

I slowly drop my bag onto the floor and turn around, seeing a giant wolf inches away from my face. The wolf is taller than I am; its head is leant down so I can see into its stunning blue eyes. They remind me of my own eyes, to be honest, with little swirls of black, light and dark blues, all mixed together. My body and mind seem to relax as I stare at the creature, one which I should be terrified of... but I am not. I feel myself moving my hand up, and then the wolf growls a little, shaking me out of that thought.

I step back, which only seems to piss her or him off more. Some deep part of me knows I have to touch the wolf now, or I will always regret it. I take a deep breath before stepping closer and quickly placing my hand on the middle of the wolf's forehead. I didn't notice it was my hand with the familiar mark on it until this point, until it glows so brightly purple that I have to turn my head away. When the light dims, I look back to see the black wolf staring at me as I lower my hand.

"Your name is Shadow," I say out loud, though I don't have a clue how I know that, but I know it is true. Shadow bows his head before lying on the ground in front of me. He is my familiar. *That's how I know.* That's why I am not scared of the enormous wolf like I should be. I have a gigantic wolf for my familiar. *Holy crap.* It takes me a few seconds to pull my gaze from Shadow and remember what I was going to do. Find my sister, that's what.

"We need to find my sister...can you help me? Like smell her, maybe? She smells like me," I ask Shadow and then realise I have no clue if he can understand me. Shadow looks up, tilting his head to the side before stretching out, knocking his head into my stomach. I step back, sighing. "Never mind."

Shadow growls at me, and I give him a questioning look. What is up with the growling? I thought familiar animals were meant to be familiars' best friends or something. I really get the feeling Shadow isn't all that impressed with me. He shakes his giant head before walking around me and slowly running off in the direction of the other building.

"Wait up!" I have to run fast to catch up with him as he gets to the front of the university, people moving fast out of his way and some even screaming. I don't even blame them. A giant black wolf running towards you is not something you see every day. I run faster, getting to Shadow's side as we round a corner, and I hear Bethany's laugh just before I see her sat on a bench with a guy. They both turn with wide, scared eyes to us, and the guy falls back off the bench before running away.

The sounds of people's screaming, shouting and general fear drift into nothing but silence as I meet my sister's eyes as she stands up. A tear streams down her cheek, saying everything neither one of us can speak. I will be made to leave her, and I have no idea when—if ever—I will get to see her again. Bethany is the first to move, running to me and wrapping her arms around my shoulders. She doesn't even look at Shadow; she doesn't fear me either, which is a huge relief. I hug her back, trying to commit every part of her to my memory as I try not to cry. *I have to be strong.* If I break down now,

Bethany will never be able to cope. I pull back as I hear sirens in the background and know my time here is coming to an end.

"I will find a way back to you. I will never stop until I do. Just look after yourself and Phoebe. Promise me?" I ask Bethany, holding my hands on her shoulders as she sobs.

"I promise. If anyone can work out a way around the rules, it's you. I love you, sis," she says, crying her eyes out between each word. I hug her once more before stepping back to Shadow's side, away from my sister and my old life. "Be safe."

"Go. Just go, I don't want you to see me arrested or how nasty the police are to familiars. The YouTube videos are enough," I say, but Bethany shakes her head, wiping her cheeks and crossing her arms. I've accidently seen enough videos online to know that the police, the government and the general population are not nice to new familiars. That's why they are taken straight away. I'm not going to fight or try to run like some familiars do. I doubt I would get far with Shadow at my side.

"I am staying until they take you. You will not be alone," she says as I hear shouting and the sounds of dozens of feet running towards us. I gasp as I feel a sharp prick in the side of my neck, and Bethany screams. Shadow growls, which turns into a howl as I try to reach for him as he falls to the ground at my side. The world turns to blackness, and the last thing I hear is Bethany's pleas for someone to leave me alone.

THE MISSING WOLF

NEW LIFE. NEW WORLD.

I cough as I wake up, my throat feeling dry and scratchy as I look up at the wood ceiling above me. The smell of fire and smoke fills my nose, making me lift my hand to rub it as I sit up. A red blanket falls to my lap as I look around the cabin I am in. Shadow is lying on the floor near a window, his eyes watching me closely, and the rest of the room is just a row of beds like the one I am in. There is a fireplace on the far wall, where the smell of burning wood is coming from. I look out the window Shadow is lying under, seeing frost covered trees. It wasn't frosty in Liverpool the last time I checked. Where have they taken me? Surely, I haven't slept the entire way to the Familiar Empire...but the evidence is looking like that is likely.

I slip my legs out of the bed, seeing that I'm still wearing the clothes from my first day at university, but they are wrinkled now, and the jeans are dirty with mud. There is a glass of water on the bedside unit and a little note. I pick the water up and take a sip before drinking it all quickly once I realise how thirsty I am. I put the glass down and pick up the note, hastily reading it.

Welcome to your new home, the Familiar Empire. The door by the fireplace leads to a bathroom, and a spare outfit is in there for you from your suitcase. Clean up and come outside. R.

I put the note back down and stare over at Shadow, remembering Bethany's pleas before the police—I presume—knocked me out. There is no going back now. I'm a familiar, and my life as I knew it is over. Grandma Pops always said you have to make the best of a bad situation because giving up is not an option. That is what I am going to do. I can fix this...*somehow*. I slide off the bed, walking past Shadow, who watches my every movement before getting to the door near the fireplace. I push it and walk inside, closing the door behind me.

The bathroom smells of bleach, but I guess that means it's clean at least. It's colder in here, and its basic design is something you would see in any hotel. There is a shower, towels on a shelf nearby, and a standard toilet and sink. I quickly use the toilet before washing my hands and looking around for the clothes. On a wooden laundry box in the corner is a pile of clothes, as the note mentioned. I pick them up, seeing ripped jeans and a blue jumper. This is one of my favourite jumpers, so I'm glad they picked that, especially considering the frost covered trees outside. I mentally catalogue all the clothes I have in my suitcase and know that not a lot of them are suitable for cold weather. I had saved up money for college, and there was little else left. Plus, Bethany assured me she had winter clothes I could borrow. *Dammit.* There is also a pink bra and matching knickers under the pile. I don't want to know who went through my suitcase and picked these; I can only hope it was a girl. By the simple fact they are a matching set, I'm willing to bet it was.

I put the clothes back and carefully pull off my dirt covered clothes. I leave them all in a pile by the sink, and as I glance up, I see my reflection in the small mirror. My hair is messy, sticking in all directions, and my skin is pale. There are big bags under my eyes, even though I've clearly slept for a long time, and my blue eyes now only remind me of Shadow and how similar they are.

I grip the sink, looking down and breathing in deep breaths. I'm a familiar. I wish I had learnt more about their kind growing up, but I never suspected I would be one of them. Only 0.003 percent of the entire human race are. *What are the chances I would be one of them?* I breathe in and shake my head once again. I know I need to shower and face the world I am now a part of. I only have to make my shaky legs move first.

It takes a few seconds before I can let go of the sink and walk the few steps to the shower. I step back as I switch it on, knowing there is a good chance cold water is going to come out first. Knowing me, I'd end up jumping back and knocking myself out somehow. I put my hand out and test the water, waiting for it to go warm before finally stepping in. Resting my head under the warm water, I let it soothe me before opening my eyes, seeing hotel-like little bottles on a shelf in front of me. I'm curious about this place, so I quickly wash my hair and myself before getting out the shower.

Lacking a hair dryer and my brush, I towel dry my hair as much as possible before running my fingers through it. It feels good to pull my clean clothes on, and I fold the towels up, not wanting to leave a mess. Going back to the mirror, I glance at myself one more time, knowing I need to walk out of here with my head lifted high. I'm Anastasia Noble, and I am familiar. The more I repeat it, the more it sinks in. This is my life now.